Matteo was holding her close. Krystiana's hands lay wet and warm upon his chest.

And suddenly she realized she was staring into his eyes, and he into hers, and their bodies were touching, and she gazed up at his lips, studded with water droplets, and she realized, intensely, that she wanted to kiss them so very much. The realization hit her with the force of a wave and she glanced up at his eyes to gauge what he was thinking and thought she saw the same desire in his gaze, too.

The desire, the need, to kiss him was just so strong, and as they closed the gap between them, inching ever closer, infinitesimally, she felt her heart pound and the blood roar around her body as if in triumph.

He'll hurt you. Everybody hurts you.

She silenced the voice. Not wanting to hear that. Not in this moment. Not right now. All she wanted right now was for…

His lips touched hers and she sank against him, feeling her body come alive.

Dear Reader,

I think most people can relate to having a trauma of some kind in their past, no matter how big or how small. It shapes some. Weakens a few. But others find a *strength* from it. It fuels them to carry on and to keep fighting every day.

I strongly believe that having a positive mental attitude, in a lot of situations, can help someone get through whatever it is. The belief that there *is* an end to it. That there *is* sunshine after the clouds go away.

Krystiana and Matteo have both experienced stormy days and this trauma brings them together and unites them in ways they couldn't possibly imagine.

I do hope you enjoy their story as much as I enjoyed writing it!

Love,

Louisa xxx

THE PRINCE'S
CINDERELLA DOC

———

LOUISA HEATON

HARLEQUIN® MEDICAL ROMANCE™

Recycling programs
for this product may
not exist in your area.

ISBN-13: 978-1-335-64149-6

The Prince's Cinderella Doc

First North American Publication 2019

Copyright © 2019 by Louisa Heaton

Printed in U.S.A.

Books by Louisa Heaton

Harlequin Medical Romance

The Baby That Changed Her Life
His Perfect Bride?
A Father This Christmas?
One Life-Changing Night
Seven Nights with Her Ex
Christmas with the Single Dad
Reunited by Their Pregnancy Surprise
Their Double Baby Gift
Pregnant with His Royal Twins
A Child to Heal Them
Saving the Single Dad Doc
Their Unexpected Babies

Visit the Author Profile page at Harlequin.com.

To Becca, with all my love. You are the strongest
young woman I know xxx

CHAPTER ONE

FOR YEARS DR KRYSTIANA SZENAC had walked along the beach with her dog Bruno, allowing her gaze to fall upon the faraway façade of Il Palazzo Grande—the Grand Palace. It was like a fine jewel in the warm sunshine. A glittering building set atop a hill, with every window, every white wall, reflecting the light. She'd often wondered about what it would be like to live in such a place, but had never imagined for one moment that she would ever pass through the arched gates into the royal sanctuary where the King and his son the Crown Prince lived.

He didn't know it, but she felt a kinship with the Prince, and every time she thought about their connection—which was often—she would smile to herself, knowing it was ridiculous because he didn't even know she existed!

But he was about to.

Krystiana sucked in a breath as the large armoured car drove her through the gates and into the palace grounds. She gazed out of the window, feeling like a silly little tourist as she took in the guards in their dark blue uniforms and the white sashes that crossed their chests, the flower displays—perfectly tended, not a weed in place—and the architecture: solid white walls rising high, the crenelated roof with the billowing flag of the royal family and the circular towers in each corner.

It had all the hallmarks of the castle it had once been, even down to the other guards she saw at the top of each tower, ever watchful, even though there had been no threat to Isla Tamoura for hundreds of years. It was pomp and circumstance for the tourists who flocked to the island in their droves, keen to explore this jewel off Italy's south-eastern coast.

Did Crown Prince Matteo feel safe behind these walls? She couldn't see why he wouldn't. All the barriers… All the guards… Security was high. She'd already had her bags searched before she was even allowed in the car. A rugged, dark-suited secret service agent had frisked her down too—the most bodily contact she'd had in years.

It had made her feel uncomfortable, but she'd bitten her lip until it was done and then smiled politely at the agent as he'd opened the car door for her. *'Grazie.'*

The agent hadn't said much. He'd had that

mysterious, moody, steely exterior down perfectly, getting into the car and saying into his phone in Italian, 'I have the parcel. Delivering in fifteen minutes—that's fifteen minutes.'

She'd raised her eyebrows, having never been referred to as a parcel before. She'd been called a lot of other things in her life, but never a *parcel*.

The car purred its way through another set of arches and then came to rest outside a columned terrace. The agent got out, adjusted the buttons on the front of his dark suit and looked about him before opening her door.

Krystiana stepped out, her nerves getting the better of her at last, and wished she'd had something to eat before leaving home. Just something that would have settled her stomach. But there'd been almost no time to prepare. The call had come in unexpectedly. She was needed immediately. There had just been time to pack a bag for an overnight stay. To call her neighbour and ask her to feed and walk Bruno.

A day of living in the palace! It was almost a dream. That a woman like her—a woman who had been raised initially in Krakow, Poland—should find herself hobnobbing with royalty.

Well, it wasn't exactly hobnobbing. It was work. Standing in for the royal doctor to run the Crown Prince through his yearly physical. She'd been chosen because she shared a clinic with Dr Bonetti, the King's private physician, and had already had her background checked. That was what happened when your colleague was the King's doctor. There could be no chance of any impropriety connected with the royals.

They'd already had enough excitement, after all.

A red carpet led from the car up to the white stone steps and into the palace proper.

On wobbly legs she ascended the stairs, aware that the agent was following along behind her. She assumed someone else would bring her bag. As she neared the top of the steps and saw the opulent interior of the palace she felt her pulse quicken, and her mouth went as dry as the Dune Dorate—the Golden Dunes.

She tried her hardest to appear nonchalant as she walked across the marble floor towards a man dressed like a butler, who had the rigid stature of an old soldier.

'Dr Szenac, welcome to the Grand Palace. It is a pleasure to welcome you to these halls. My name is Sergio and I shall be your attendant whilst you are here. Have you been to the palace before?'

She shook her head, her long golden plait swinging at her back. 'No. It's my first time.'

'Oh! Well, please don't let it be your last. I'm reliably informed that the public tours are very entertaining and informative, if you wish to know anything of its history.'

She'd never been one to study history. History should stay in the past, where it belonged. Not be dragged back into the present at every opportunity. She could appreciate beautiful architecture, and respect the amount of time a building had stood in place, but she was far more interested in the people who lived in it now.

'Thank you. I might do that one day.'

Sergio led her up a curved stairwell, adorned with portraiture of Kings and Queens of the past. She could see the familiar glossy black hair and beautiful blue eyes of the Romano family in most of them. Occasionally there was a portrait of someone who had married into the family, including the one she stood in front of now: Queen Marianna, sadly passed.

'She was beautiful, wasn't she?' asked Sergio.

'Most definitely.'

'And not just in looks. She had a very kind heart. It broke her when her son was taken. She died never knowing of his safe return.'

Krystiana nodded. It was tragic. Crown Prince Matteo's kidnapping had been a story she had followed with bated breath, praying for his safe release. It had been a couple of years ago now, but still, she knew in her heart that it would never be forgotten by those involved.

'The Prince must have been devastated when he got home to discover his mother had died?'

Sergio nodded sadly. 'They were very close. Ah, here are your quarters.'

He stopped in front of a set of double doors and swung them open wide, and once again she tried to appear unaffected by the riches within, simply nodding and smiling.

'Thank you, Sergio. These look wonderful. I'm sure I'll be very comfortable.'

'Your initial appointment with the Prince is at three this afternoon. Take time to settle in. Pull this red sash—' he indicated a brocade sash that hung by the white marble fireplace '—if you want anything and I'll be with you momentarily.'

'Thank you.'

'A servant will bring up your bag. Are there any refreshments I can get you? A drink, perhaps?'

She *was* thirsty, and now that some of her nerves were settling she felt that maybe she could eat. 'Some coffee would be wonderful. And some water? Maybe a bite to eat? I had to come here in rather a rush and I'm afraid I didn't get a chance to dine.'

'I'll have a selection of food brought up to you immediately. Do you have any allergies or food preferences?'

'No.'

He bowed. 'Then I will be back shortly. Welcome to the Grand Palace, Doctor.' And he departed, closing the doors behind him.

Krystiana spun around, headed straight over to the doors in the far wall and flung them back, allowing in the bright sunshine, the freedom of the outdoors, as she stepped out onto a large terrace and breathed in the scent of bougainvillea, jasmine and columbine.

An array of flowers grew in small ornamental pots, framed by clipped firs in taller blue pots. A table and six chairs were sheltered by a large umbrella. Below her were the private royal gardens and she took a moment to take in the sight. They were simply gorgeous: a low maze with a water feature at its centre—a stone horse crashing through stone waves—an ornamental garden, a lily pond, a mosaic. Little paths ran here and there—one down to a grotto, another through a set of rose arches to a circular bench and a bust.

Someone had poured a lot of heart and soul into this garden. She wondered who. Some gardener? A series of them? Each of them adding something new during their term, perhaps?

Beyond the palace walls she saw olive groves, small terracotta-coloured churches, roadside shrines and undulating hillsides that shimmered with heat from the overhead sun. It was something she could paint. She often turned to creativity when she was stressed. She'd never had such a view before—she *had* to sketch it before she left.

Not that I could ever forget this.

The view had a timeless quality. She almost felt she could stand there all day admiring it. But reality beckoned, and so she turned to observe her rooms more carefully. It was the most sumptuous suite—all white marble and silver accents. A large bed occupied the centre of the bedroom, with pristine white sheets and a gold counterpane. There was a desk and chair in the living room, a comfortable pair of sofas in palest cornflower-blue and vases of fresh flowers on almost every surface. A door in the corner of the bedroom led to an en-suite bathroom, with a sunken bath in the centre, a walk-in shower, a toilet and bidet and a huge assortment of toiletries in a room that was all mirrors.

Briefly, she wondered about the poor maids who had to clean it each day, buffing it to a shine, because not a single surface had a fingerprint or a smudge on it anywhere.

But what would you expect in a palace?

The opulence was meant to make her feel good. Treasured and important. But Krystiana had always preferred simplicity and rustic touches. Wooden bowls, plain knives and forks for her food. Simple cloth mats beneath her plate.

Watercolours. Plain whitewashed walls—the minimalist look, with stone and driftwood she'd collected from the beach where she walked each day, barefoot, her trousers rolled up as she paddled in the water.

All of this was nice. Amazing, in fact. But it wasn't real.

She felt like Alice through the looking glass, looking at a world she didn't quite understand. But she was keen to know more.

Crown Prince Matteo Romano shook the hand of the cultural attaché from Portugal and bade him a safe journey home. He was looking forward to the future visit he would take to Lisbon, to see for himself the amazing artwork said to be displayed in Galleria 111. The attaché had done a fine job of convincing him the place was worth fitting in to his schedule, especially as he was such a fan of the surrealist painter António Dacosta, the work of whom the gallery had confirmed they had a huge stock.

As soon as the attaché had left, Matteo let out a breath and relaxed for a moment. He was almost done with his schedule for today. A few brief moments alone, and then he would meet the new doctor who had been brought in due to Dr Bonetti's family emergency.

He hoped everything was all right with the

man's family. He'd known Dr Bonetti for years, and had met his wife and children. They'd all dined together on occasion and he thought very well of them all. He envied the doctor his happy marriage and his smiling children. They all seemed so *together*. So...*content*.

None of them had the stresses that were placed upon *his* shoulders. Who could understand the burden of being a prince, a future king, without having lived in his shoes?

He reached for the coffee that Sergio had brought in earlier, along with the news that the stand-in doctor had arrived and was settling in. The drink was cooler than he'd like—his meeting with the Portuguese attaché had gone on longer than he'd expected—but he continued to drink it until it was finished. Then, needing the freshness of the outdoors and the calm that viewing the gardens gave him, he stepped out of the terrace doors onto the balcony to gaze down into the palace gardens.

As always, he felt serenity begin to settle in his soul and he closed his eyes and breathed in the warm, fragrant air. *Perfezionare*. Perfect. His hands came to rest on the rich stone balustrade and for a moment he just stood there, centring himself. Grounding himself.

Behind him there was the gentle sound of Sergio clearing his throat. 'Dr Krystiana Szenac, sir.'

'*Grazie*, Sergio.'

He turned and there she was. Dressed in a black knee-length skirt and an emerald-green blouse, her blonde hair flowing over her shoulder in a long plait. A hint of make-up and an amazing smile.

She curtsied. 'Your Highness.'

'Dr Szenac. It's a pleasure.' He stepped forward to shake her hand. 'I appreciate you coming at short notice and hope our pulling you from your schedule hasn't disrupted your life too much.'

'No. Not at all. I was able to make new arrangements. When your country calls, you answer.'

He smiled. 'Indeed. I take it your journey was uneventful?'

'It was wonderful, thank you.'

'And Dr Bonetti?'

'His wife has been taken into emergency surgery, but I'm afraid that's all I know.'

Emergency surgery? That didn't sound good.

'Let us hope she pulls through. Alexis Bonetti is a strong woman—I'm sure her constitution will hold her in good stead.'

She nodded. 'I hope so.'

'May I offer you a refreshment before we settle down?'

'I'm fine, thank you. Sergio had some coffee brought to my room.'

'Excellent.'

He stared at her for a moment more and then indicated that maybe they should sit down at one of the tables on the sun terrace. He pulled out a chair for her, and she smiled her thanks at him as she sat down.

He sat opposite. 'Well, I'll try not to keep you here too long. I just need my yearly physical to be carried out. Dr Bonetti usually does the deed, but this year it will be down to you—if that's all right?'

'Absolutely.'

'He usually runs a barrage of tests—I'm sure there's a list somewhere. And then, if I'm all okay, he signs me off for another year.'

'I know what to do—don't worry. He emailed me your file, with a list of assessments I need to put you through and the paperwork that needs filling out.' Dr Szenac smiled. 'According to your file you're in very good health, and your last couple of physicals had you back at full health after your…' she looked uncomfortable '…blip.'

'My *kidnapping*. Yes. Well… Two years in a cave, will do that to any man.'

She nodded. 'Yes. My apologies for bringing it up.'

'Not at all. My therapist says it's good to talk about it. The more often the better.'

She smiled her thanks.

He didn't want her to feel uncomfortable, so he tried to change the subject. 'You're originally from Poland?'

'Yes. Krakow.'

'I've never been there. What's it like?'

'I don't know. I haven't been there for years. I just remember the grey and the cold.'

He saw her shiver and it intrigued him that she could still feel it, all these years later, just *thinking* about it.

'When did you move here?'

'When my mother died. My father was…away, and I had no one else except for my Aunt Carolina, who lives here.'

'On Isla Tamoura?'

'Yes.'

'Well, I'm very glad you're here.' He smiled.

She nodded. 'Yes. Me too.'

CHAPTER TWO

WHEN KRYSTIANA WOKE the next morning, the first thing she did was reach over and turn off her night-light. It was an automatic thing—something she hardly noticed doing—but today when she did so she stared at it for a moment, wondering if Crown Prince Matteo had one too.

For two years he'd been stuck in a cave. Was he now afraid of the dark?

Throwing off the bedcovers, she got up and threw open the double doors to the sun terrace. The fragrant air poured in and she closed her eyes for a moment as the warm rays from the sun caressed her skin. This was what she loved about living here. The warmth. The colour. The heat. The beauty of this treasured isle.

How fortunate that her aunt lived here. It had been exactly what she had needed after her experience at the hands of her father—to leave such an ugly existence behind and come to a place that only had beauty at its core. There had been a new language to learn, but wonderful, loving, passionate people to support her. New friends. A new life. Isla Tamoura had given her a new beginning, a new hope, and she loved it here so much.

Krystiana took a quick shower and braided her long hair into its usual plait, donned a summery dress and sat down to eat the breakfast that had been brought in on a tray. She was used to eating breakfast alone. She quite enjoyed it. But this time, before her day started, she grabbed her pad and pencils and began sketching the view from her balcony. This afternoon she would be going home again, so there was no time to spare.

Her sketch was vague. Outlines and shapes. She would fill in the colour later, allowing her imagination to take flight. She took a couple of quick photos using her phone.

She almost lost track of time, and when she did glance at her watch she saw there were only a few minutes until nine o clock—her scheduled time to give the Prince his yearly physical. She left her pad and pencil on the bed, finished her orange juice and then pulled the sash to call Sergio. She wasn't sure exactly where in the palace the examination would take place.

Sergio arrived, looking as perfectly presented as always. 'Good morning, Dr Szenac. I hope you slept well?'

'Very well, Sergio, thank you. I have my appointment with His Highness Prince Matteo, to start his physical, but I'm not sure where I have to go.'

He nodded. 'I believe you are expected in the private gym. Dr Bonetti always carries out the yearly check-ups there.'

'Thank you.' She'd had no idea the palace had its own gym—but, then again, why wouldn't it? Matteo and his family could hardly pop out to the local leisure centre if they wanted to lift a few weights, could they?

Sergio led her through the palace, down long tapestry-filled hallways, past vast vases so big she could have climbed inside and not been seen even standing upright. They passed a coat of arms, a suit of armour, and fireplaces filled with flowers, until he brought her to a set of double doors.

'The gym, Dr Szenac. All of Dr Bonetti's equipment has been laid out for you, and the computer has been set up for you to enter the results of each test for the record.'

'Thank you—that's very kind.'

'The computer isn't likely to be difficult, but if you do have any queries we have an IT expert on hand.'

'That's marvellous.'

Sergio smiled and opened the doors.

The gym was filled with all types of equipment—treadmills, stair-masters, weight machines, free-standing weights, workout equipment, yoga mats. Anything and everything seemed to be here, and one wall was made of glass that revealed a room beyond filled with a full-length swimming pool.

Pretty impressive!

But she didn't have time to linger. The Prince would be here at any moment and she wanted to be prepared.

She was running her eye over what she needed to achieve today, reminding herself of the assessments, when she became aware of a presence behind her.

'Dr Szenac.'

She turned and bowed slightly. 'Your Highness.'

'I'm ready, if you are?'

Smiling, she nodded. 'Absolutely. Ready to begin with the basics? I'll need to do blood pressure, pulse and SATs.'

'Perfect.'

'All right. Take a seat.'

She began to set up her equipment—the pulse oximeter that she'd place on his finger to measure not only his pulse but the oxygen levels in his blood, and the arm cuff around his upper arm that would measure his blood pressure.

His basic measurements were perfect. Exactly what she'd expected them to be.

'Okay, now I need to check your height and weight.'

'I don't think I've shrunk.'

She smiled. 'Glad to hear it.'

Again, his weight was perfect for his height.

'Now I'd like to set you up for a treadmill test. I'll need to attach you to a breathing tube, so we can measure oxygen intake, heart-rate and lung capacity whilst you run up a slight incline for three minutes.'

He nodded. 'Can I warm up first?'

'By all means.'

She looked at his previous measurements and typed them into the computer, aware that Matteo was stripping off behind her and beginning to stretch.

When she turned around she noted that he was in excellent physical shape. Clearly he used the gym often to keep fit. His muscle tone was almost beautiful. His figure was sculpted, without being overly worked. It seemed almost wrong to look at him and admire him like that. Not least because he was a prince.

'Right, I need to attach these electrodes, if that's okay?'

Does my voice sound weird?

He stood still whilst she attached the electrodes to his chest and body, trying her hardest not to make eye contact, then attached the wires that hooked him up to the machine for a reading. She fastened a breathing mask around his nose and mouth, and suddenly there was that eye contact thing.

She could feel herself blushing. 'Okay... For the first minute I want you just to walk at a steady pace and then, when I tell you, I'm going to increase the speed and I want you to jog.'

'All right.'

'Ready?'

He gave her a thumbs-up and she started the treadmill and the EKG monitor that would read his heart's electrical activity. The machine began printing out on a paper roll and she watched it steadily, keeping a careful eye out for any issues, but it all looked fine.

She glanced up at him as he ran with a steady pace, his body like a well-oiled machine as he tackled the jog easily. His oxygen intake was perfect; his heart-rate was elevated, but not too much.

When the three minutes were over she switched everything off and then laid a hand on his wrist to check his pulse. She felt it pounding away beneath her fingertips and kept count, then made a note of the result.

'You're doing brilliantly.'

He pulled off the mask. 'Good to know.'

'You work out a lot?'

'Can't you tell?' He raised an eyebrow.

'Well, I…er…yes… You look very…er…'

He laughed. 'I meant can't you tell from my results?'

She flushed even redder and laughed with him. 'Oh, I see.' She nodded. 'Yes!'

'I try to do thirty minutes every other day, alternating with the pool. Lifting weights. Half an hour of cardio…'

'You do more than me.'

'It's easier for me. My life is scheduled to the minute, so I know when I can fit things in to get everything done.'

She was curious. 'Is that a perk or a drawback?' she asked. She wasn't sure she'd want to be so regimentally scheduled each day. What about free time? What about spontaneity?

'It depends on the day.' He laughed again, wiping his face with a towel.

'And today?'

He shrugged. 'Well, I have this, and then I get to spend some time with my daughter.'

'Princess Alexandra? She's beautiful. How old is she now?'

'Five.'

'You must be very proud of her.'

'I am. But I don't get to spoil her as often as I would like.'

Of course not. She didn't live with him. The Princess lived with her mother, at her family's private estate.

'That must be hard for you?'

He stared into her eyes. 'You have no idea.'

Oh, but I do, she thought. *I know how hard it is being away from those you love. I know only too well.*

She blinked rapidly and turned away, forcing her mind back to the assessment. 'Next test.'

'I'm all yours.' He did a mock bow.

Krystiana smiled and then indicated that he should move to the next machine.

They were just about finished with their testing when the doors to the gym opened and in walked Sergio, looking grave. It was the most solemn Matteo had ever seen him.

He finished towelling himself down and raised an eyebrow. 'Sergio? What is it?'

'I have some unfortunate news for Dr Szenac, sir.'

She looked up from her notes and frowned. Was it about Dr Bonetti's wife?

'I'm afraid there's been an accident at your villa. A drunk driver tried to take the corner near your abode too fast and ploughed into your home. I'm afraid your living area and bedroom have been almost destroyed, and the property is not safe for you to reside in just yet.'

Matteo was shocked and looked to Dr Szenac. 'I'm so sorry!'

Her face was almost white. 'Is the driver all right?'

He was impressed at how her concern was immediately for the driver.

'I believe he got away quite lightly, all things considered. He's being treated by the medics now.'

'Okay. Good. That's good.' She turned away, her thoughts in a distant place. 'Oh, my God. What about Bruno?'

'Bruno?'

'My dog. He's a rescue.'

'I believe your neighbour was out on a walk with him at the time,' Sergio replied.

'Oh, thank goodness!'

She sank down into a chair, her legs obviously trembling, and put her head in her hands. Matteo felt for her. Was her home ruined?

'You must stay here with us. Until everything is fixed.'

She looked up, tears in her eyes. 'I couldn't possibly do that.'

'Nonsense! It's done. Sergio, could you arrange for Dr Szenac's clothes and anything she needs to be brought to her quarters here in the palace? Including her dog, who I'm sure will bring her great comfort. We're going to have a guest for a while.'

'I don't know what to say…' she said, beginning to cry.

He smiled. 'Say yes.'

She looked at him for a long moment and he saw gratitude. 'Then, yes. Thank you. Yes.'

He nodded. 'Sergio? Make it happen.'

'I'm so lucky I was here when it happened, she said later. Otherwise I might have been injured!'

'Well, you were here, and that's all that matters.'

'But—'

'No buts. There's no point in wondering about what *might* have happened. You just need to worry about what *is* happening.' He smiled. 'I learned that in therapy. Look at me—spreading the knowledge.'

She smiled as she stroked Bruno's fur. They'd had a joyous reunion when Sergio had returned with her dog, her clothes, her computer and some rather startling photographs of the damage to her villa.

'That's going to take weeks to repair,' she'd said.

'Let me take care of that,' Matteo had offered.

'I couldn't possibly let you do that! It will cost a fortune!'

'Are you insured?'

'Yes.'

'Then don't worry about it. Let me do something good for you. You were kind enough to step in at the last minute and help me out when I needed a doctor—let me step in and help you out when you need a...'

'A builder?' She'd laughed.

He'd smiled back. 'A knight in shining armour. Didn't you see my suit of armour downstairs? It's very polished.'

So of course she'd thanked him profusely, feeling so terribly grateful for all that he was doing to help her out.

'I appreciate that. I really do.'

'Nonsense. It's what friends do.'

And she'd smiled. *Were they friends?* 'Thank you.'

Matteo had invited her to dine with him that evening.

'You can bring Bruno. If he's lucky we might be able to feed him titbits under the table.'

'He'll never want to leave this place if you do that.'

And now they sat on his sun terrace, awaiting

their meal, staring out across the gardens below and watching the sun slowly set.

'By the way, I don't know if you've heard but Dr Bonetti's wife has pulled through. She's in a stable condition and expected to go home soon. He phoned from the hospital. Let my secretary know.'

'That's excellent news! Wow. So good to have such great news after earlier. And the driver who hit my home? Do we know about him?'

'Already home. And already charged by the police for drink driving. He's to attend court in a few days' time.'

'If it was an accident I'm sure he's very sorry.'

Matteo sipped his water. 'Unfortunately, from what I've discovered, the man is a known drunk. He's already had his licence taken from him and the car wasn't even his. It was his son's and he'd "borrowed" it.'

'Oh.'

'We'll get him into a programme.'

'We?' She raised an eyebrow.

'My pack of royal enforcers,' he said with a straight face, knowing there was no such pack at all.

'Enforcers?'

He laughed. 'I'm sorry. I don't really have enforcers. I was just… Look, he needs help. Someone will go and visit him and make sure he enrols into a programme that will get him the help he needs. Before he kills someone next time.'

'Maybe I could go and see him myself?'

'Is that wise? You're emotionally involved.'

'Which is why he might listen to me. Meeting the actual victim of his crime might make more of an impact.'

'Was hitting your wall not enough?' He cocked his head to one side. 'How do you know so much about crime and victimology?'

She looked down and away from him then, and he realised there was a story there. Something she wasn't willing to share.

'I'm sorry—you don't have to answer that.'

She laughed. 'Don't therapists suggest that talking is good for the soul?'

He nodded. 'They do. But only when you're ready. *Are* you ready?'

'I don't know.'

He sipped his drink. 'You'll know when it's the right time. And, more importantly, if it's the right person to talk to. You don't really know me, so I quite understand.'

She stared back at him. Consideringly. Her eyes were cool. 'I think you'd understand more than most.'

He considered this. Intrigued. 'Oh?'

She paused. Looked uncertain. And then he

saw it in her face. The determination to push forward and just say it.

'I was six years old. And I was taken.'

'Taken?' His blood almost froze, despite the warmth of the sun.

'My father buried me in a hole in the ground.'

CHAPTER THREE

She stared at him, trying to gauge his reaction. 'Surprised?'

The Crown Prince opened his mouth as if to say something, but no words came out. He was truly stupefied. Shocked. His mind raced over the fact that she'd been kidnapped too.

'Of course I am! Your *father* did this?'

'He planned it. It wasn't a spur-of-the-moment thing. My parents had split up and had a bitter custody battle over me. Their divorce was not amicable.'

'That must have been upsetting for you.'

A nod. 'Yes. My mother was awarded full custody, but my father got to see me once a month. Just for one day. This particular weekend he told me we were going to play a game in the woods, where he worked as a gamekeeper. I was going to help him snare rabbits.'

Matteo listened intently, his face showing how

appalled he was that something like this had happened to her.

'We went deep into the woods. It was dark and damp and there almost wasn't any light… the trees were so thick.'

'Were you scared?'

'Not to start with. I was comfortable being in nature. I'd played in those woods. I was with my father. I thought I was safe. And then he showed me a bunker he'd made.'

'A bunker…? What was it like?'

'Not very big. Maybe the size of a single bed? The walls were lined with wood. Old pallets, I think. He told me we were going to play a game, and that to play I had to get inside the bunker and wait whilst he went and chased rabbits towards it. He told me the roof would open easily. That I'd be able to push it open and the rabbits would jump into the dark for me to play with.'

'Mio Dio…'

'Once he put the roof down I heard a padlock click. He said *"Przepraszam"*—I'm sorry—and then he left me.'

She took a sip of water, reliving that moment once again in her mind, hearing her father's footsteps as he walked away and how it felt for her tiny fists to beat against the solid roof above her head, lined with soil.

'He would come back when he could, to bring

me food and water. I tried to escape, but…he was stronger than me. Once he brought a book and a candle, so I had light to read.'

'How long were you underground?'

'Six weeks.'

He looked sick. 'How did you escape?'

'I was found. My father had reported me missing, of course. Said I'd disappeared when he'd left me outside a shop. After a few weeks the police began to suspect him and followed him into the woods. Dogs found me. I'll always remember hearing them come closer, their barks echoing above me. I began to scream. I screamed so much I had no voice for three days.'

'And your father?'

She swallowed hard. 'He's in prison now.'

He nodded. 'Do you visit him?'

Why did he not know about this? She worked with his father's doctor! How come none of this had shown in her background searches?

Because she'd been a child. The records would be sealed.

'No. I've never gone back to Poland.'

'Do you think you should?'

Her head tilted to one side as she assessed him. 'Have you ever visited your captors in jail?'

Matteo thought for a moment, then smiled, caught out. 'Fair point. But my captors were strangers—yours was your father. You must have loved him?'

'I did. But not any more. It's not the same.'

'And…' He cleared his throat and took a sip of water. 'Do you have any flashbacks? Any issues from your captivity?'

'Not really. Apart from needing a night-light.'

'That's understandable.' He looked out at the broad expanse of rich orange-pink sky, cloudless and still.

'So, Your Highness, as you can see we are both injured birds.'

'I guess we are. But we're resilient and we'll both fly again.'

She looked uncertain. 'I hope I already am flying.'

He nodded. 'You are. Believe it.'

She smiled back, thankful for his understanding and support. Who'd have thought it? That she'd be sharing her story with the Crown Prince?

How many times had she gazed at these palace walls, wanting to let him know that she understood what he had gone through? How many times had she considered writing him a letter but decided against it? Assuming that he wouldn't actually see it, and that it would be dealt with by a private secretary.

They were probably the only two people on

this island who shared such an experience. It
bonded them. And here she was. Sitting across
from him, watching the sunset, sharing with him
her darkest nightmare.

'You're a good man, Your Highness.'

He smiled back at her, his blue eyes twinkling.
'Call me Matteo.'

She nodded. 'Krystiana.'

She lay on her bed, staring at the ceiling. Had she
been a fool to blurt it out like that? She'd never
told anyone here about what had happened. Only
her Aunt Carolina knew—no one else. Until
today, anyway. She hadn't even told Dr Bonetti,
and he was her partner in the medical practice
they ran in the town of Ventura.

But sitting opposite Matteo like that, being
that close to him, she had wanted him to know.
It was as simple as that. Being kidnapped was
such a unique experience, and she'd needed him
to know that she understood it. That she'd been
through it, too.

He'd been so kind.

'Thank you, Krystiana. For sharing that with
me,' he had said. 'It must have taken great courage to share something so…personal.'

She'd pushed her *tagliatelli* around her plate,
biting her bottom lip. Trying to work out why
she'd told him everything. Was she being selfish?

'I've kept it inside for so long… It felt good to get it out. I guess I knew you'd understand.'

She'd looked up, expecting to see sympathy or pity on his face, but he hadn't looked at her that way at all.

'Other people don't. Not truly,' he'd said. 'They couldn't.'

'No.' She'd sipped her water.

'I don't want you to feel bad for telling me. I can see it on your face that you're uncomfortable now.'

She'd smiled wryly at his perceptiveness. Was she an open book? Could he read her? Was she so obvious? Or was it that only he could see, because he'd been through the same thing?

She'd given a short laugh. 'I'm normally so private. I keep myself to myself. My best friend doesn't even know. There's no alcohol in this water, right?' she tried to joke.

Matteo had nodded. 'I'm honoured you shared it with me.'

Krystiana continued to stare at the bedroom ceiling. So different from the one in her villa. Back home she had a ceiling fan in the centre of the roof; here she had a chandelier, reflecting the brightness from her night-light around the room.

Her conversation with Matteo hadn't been uncomfortable because she'd shared her story with him—it had become uncomfortable because she hadn't realised what sharing it might make her *feel*. She'd entrusted him with something of herself and she didn't like it. Okay, it was only a small piece of her past, but still... If she'd told him that, what else might she say?

She felt as if she'd given him some of her power and that felt wrong. It was an unexpected emotion.

She got little sleep that night, and when she did finally wake in the morning she vowed to herself that maybe it would be a good idea to stay away from the Crown Prince for a while, He had a busy life, anyway—she probably wouldn't see him any more, and she would have to leave the palace to go to work each day at her practice and see her real patients.

She'd told him about her kidnapping because she'd often thought he would be intrigued to know, but that was as far as it went. That was all. Their lives were separate.

It was as if she was just renting a room and he was her extraordinary new landlord.

A car was waiting to take her to work. A sleek, black armoured vehicle, with its engine idling and one of those dark-suited Secret Service guys behind the wheel.

Krystiana trotted down the steps, ready for work, but also ready to drive past her old home and see the wreckage for herself first. She was anxious, her belly full of a twisting apprehension so that she hadn't been able to manage any breakfast and had only had a single cup of coffee.

'Come on, Bruno! Hurry up!' Her dog, a middle-aged pooch of indeterminate breed, with the character of a grumpy geriatric, ambled after her.

Sergio opened the car door for her. 'Have a good day, Dr Szenac.'

'*Grazie*, Sergio.' As she got into the car, she almost jumped out of her skin. 'Your Highness! What are *you* doing in here? I thought this was the car that was going to take me to work?'

He smiled. 'Matteo—remember? And good morning to you, too. I thought I would come with you to survey the damage to your house.'

'B-but...' she stuttered. 'Aren't you busy? Surely you have more important things to be getting on with? Like helping to run a country?'

'One of my citizens has had her home destroyed by a fool who should never have been on the road in the first place. I am doing my duty by attending the scene of the tragedy to see if there is anything I can do.' He leaned in. 'It's called being supportive—so accept that fact and close the door. Bruno!'

He patted his hands against his lap and her dog jumped in, up onto the car's expensive leather seats and smoothly onto the Prince's lap. He gave her a smile that was cunning and smooth, sliding his sunglasses down onto his face.

'Is that your disguise?' she asked.

'No. I have a baseball cap, too, and when we get to your villa both of us will have hard hats. The site manager will show us around.'

'They're working on it already?'

'From first light this morning.'

She pulled her legs in and Sergio shut the door behind her. 'That's impressive.'

'It's what I do.'

Krystiana smiled at him and then she laughed. He really was very kind. And going completely above and beyond anything she'd expected of him. Not that she *did* expect anything of him. He'd been her patient for one day. Now he wasn't. And, although he'd said they were friends, she wasn't sure how to negotiate that particular relationship.

She didn't have the best track record with men, and she hadn't been kidding when she'd told him she kept to herself. She'd only got one friend and that was Anna Scottolini, her next-door neighbour. She'd neglected to tell him that the best friend she'd mentioned was a senior citizen in her ninety-second year of life.

'You passed, by the way.'

'I'm sorry?'

'Your yearly physical. With flying colours. You're fit as a fiddle.'

'How fit *are* fiddles?'

She shrugged. 'Very, it would seem. Bruno! Don't be embarrassing!'

Bruno had decided the lap of the Prince was a very good place to begin washing his nether regions and had set to with gusto. Feeling her cheeks flame red, she reached over to grab the dog and pull him onto the seat between them.

'Sit there. Good dog.'

Matteo smiled at her and she felt something stir within her. Whatever it was, it made her feel incredibly uncomfortable.

Matching him, she pulled her sunglasses from her handbag and slid them over her face and turned to look out of the window.

If I don't look at him, I won't think about him. Yeah. Like that's going to work!

Krystiana's villa sat atop a small hill on the road into Ventura—or out of it, depending upon which way you were going. When Matteo stepped out of the vehicle in a simple white shirt and dark trousers, and donned his baseball cap and sunglasses, he could see the palace far in the distance, shining like a pearl. White and glittering.

He wondered briefly, now he knew exactly

where she lived, if he would be able to spot her home from the palace walls?

Because of course he would always think of her now. No matter what happened in the future, he would feel a kinship with this woman at his side because of what they'd both been through. After she'd told him what had happened he'd initially been shocked, but drawn in by her story. So similar and yet so different from his own.

Six weeks underground. Alone and in the dark.

Kindred spirits. That was what they were. So he was glad he'd made her the offer to stay at the palace whilst her home was worked on, and he did want to see the damage for himself—but had it only been that? Concern for one of his citizens? Concern for someone he'd like to think of as a friend? Or something more?

He felt at ease when he was with her. There was something relaxing about her. But that in turn worried him, simply because it *was* so easy to be with her. He could be himself—and he hadn't been himself for a very long time. It was confusing and alarming, because what did it *mean*? For so long now he'd held himself apart from everyone. Ever since he'd returned home. And yet he'd spent one day with her and had discovered that...

He turned to look at her house. At the metal

fencing around the perimeter and the crumpled mess beyond it. Because that was what it was. A crumpled mess of brick and rubble, mortar and plaster, glass and wood. He'd seen something similar when he'd once gone to help during the aftershocks of an earthquake the island had experienced a few years back.

Thank goodness she hadn't been inside when it had happened. If Dr Bonetti's wife hadn't been ill he'd have done his physical as usual and Krystiana would have been at home.

Fate? He didn't believe in that any more.

Pure luck? Maybe…

A man in a high-vis vest and a yellow hard hat came around the corner. He raised a hand and ambled slowly over the loose rubble before coming to the metal fencing and opening a panel. 'Your Highness.'

'Carlo?'

'Si.'

'This is Dr Szenac—she is the owner of this property. Could you walk us through it? Let us know what's happening?'

Carlo nodded and led the way. The ground was uneven, loose bricks and rubble everywhere, so Matteo turned to offer her his hand.

'I'm fine,' she said. 'Watch where you're going and I'll follow.'

He nodded. It was probably a good thing that

she hadn't accepted his hand. After all, he was meant to be keeping his distance.

I really must work harder on that.

Her kitchen and bathroom looked untouched by the collision, but the rest of her downstairs rooms and to some degree the rooms above had pretty much collapsed down on top of each other. The vehicle that had smacked into the villa had been a large four-wheel drive, and the driver had been going at some speed. She'd expected to see a car-shaped hole in her wall, or something, but not this. This was...*shocking*. This was the home she had built up since moving out of Aunt Carolina's...

'I'm so sorry, Krystiana,' Matteo said as they surveyed the wreckage.

She didn't want to cry. She had done her make-up for work later. Now she was going to look like a panda.

One of her sofas seemed to be missing. Some framed photographs lay on the floor, their glass cracked and missing fragments. Bending down, she went to pick one up. The only picture she had of her mother. Her eyes welled up again and she began to sob, her hand clamped over her mouth as she tried to cry silently.

'Hey, come here...' Matteo pulled her towards him and she huddled against his chest, the photograph of her dead mother in her hands.

He was warm and comforting. Soothing. And although she wanted to remain there for ever she sniffed hard and pushed away from his chest, stepping out of his arms. She couldn't. No. It wasn't right.

'I'm fine. Really. Show me everything, Carlo.'

Carlo looked at Matteo for permission and she saw him give a terse nod.

She followed him around, listened as he gave complicated observations about lintels and weight-bearing walls and nodded, pretending she understood everything he said. They couldn't go upstairs. It hadn't been made safe yet, he said. But she'd got what she needed. The one thing that mattered. There'd been no way she was leaving her mother in the rubble. In the darkness. Like a piece of discarded litter.

'Thank you. You've been very informative.'

'How long should the work take?' asked Matteo.

'If we can get the supplies we need, four weeks minimum. But it may be longer than that.'

'Do what you can. Money is no object—do you understand me?'

'Yes, Your Highness.'

Matteo turned to her. 'I'll walk you back to the car.'

And he followed her through the building site that was now her home, occasionally putting the tips of his fingers on the small of her back, guiding her through.

When they reached the car, he sighed. 'Are you all right?'

'I'm fine.'

'Maybe you shouldn't return to work today?'

'I have to. I have my own patients *and* Dr Bonetti's. I can't let them down and I won't.'

'All right. I'll have the car drop you off and then pick you up again tonight.'

She shook her head. 'You don't have to. You have work too, remember?'

Matteo nodded. 'Yes. You're right. But it seems wrong leaving you when you're upset.'

'I'll be fine. We're strong, aren't we?'

He smiled. 'We're strong. Yes.' He glanced at the back seat of the car. 'Want me to take Bruno?'

'He sits in the office with me. Patients seem to like it.' She shrugged.

'Interesting medical student…'

'He has a passion for bones.'

It was a lame joke, but she was trying to make light of the situation. It had been a stressful twenty-four hours, but she'd been through worse.

Matteo smiled dutifully. 'I'll see you at home, then.'

Home.

She got into the car, waiting for him to slide

in next to her. Bruno gave a wag of his tail and licked some dust off the back of her hand.

'Don't wait up.'

Krystiana spent the day treating patients, and for almost six hours barely gave a thought to her ruined home or her palatial sleepover. She treated an infected jellyfish sting, a child with chicken pox, two bad sunburns, a bad case of laryngitis, gout, completed a newborn baby's assessment, and checked a wound on the foot of a Type Two diabetic—all before lunch.

It felt good to get back to her normal routine, to see her patients' faces and to slide back into the routine of consulting and issuing prescriptions. There was a rhythm to it, a logic. Medicine was often a puzzle, with the patients the clues, and there was nothing she loved more than to solve the puzzle and heal the patient. Helping people was what she did best, and it made her feel good about herself that she could do so.

A therapist would no doubt say that it was down to her feeling so powerless and impotent when her father had kept her below ground. That the fact that she hadn't been able to help her mother when she died fired her soul now.

Maybe it was true. Who knew? Perhaps that was why she was so anxious to leave the palace? She'd done her thing. She'd helped out when Dr

Bonetti hadn't been able to make it and now her part was over. She wasn't needed at the palace any more, but she had to stay there because she needed a place to sleep.

Or did she? Maybe Anna, her next-door neighbour and best friend, could put her up until the work on her house was done?

No. I can't ask her to do that. She's in her nineties! And besides, how would I pay for the repairs? I'm insured, but that would take ages, and Matteo is getting the work done quicker than I ever could.

It felt wrong. He was being so generous and she wasn't used to someone helping her like that. She was used to standing on her own two feet. Being independent.

She was mulling this over when her next patient arrived. Sofia De Laurentis. Sixteen years old and the daughter of a duke. A lot of her patients came from among the upper echelons of society, but class and prestige were not enough to keep away disease.

Sofia was Krystiana's last patient of the day, and she entered her consulting room looking nervous, fidgeting with her backpack.

'Hello, Sofia, what's brought you here today?'

Sofia couldn't meet her eyes. 'You can't tell anyone, but… I think I might be pregnant.'

Krystiana didn't react. 'All right. What makes you think that?'

'My period is late. A few weeks. And I feel weird.'

Krystiana took some details. The date of her last period and how long they usually lasted. 'Have you taken a pregnancy test?'

'I bought one. I had to go in disguise—can you believe that? There were two tests inside and I used them both.'

'Positive?'

Sofia nodded.

'And do you know who the father is?'

Another nod.

And then she asked the most important question as her patient was only sixteen. 'Did you consent?'

'Yes.'

She believed her. 'Okay. Let's get you up onto the bed.'

Krystiana felt her tummy, but it was still too early to feel the fundus—the top of the womb—above her pelvic area. She smiled, and helped pull Sofia back up into a sitting position.

'Take a seat.'

She prepared to take her blood pressure, wrapping the cuff around her arm.

'So, I can take a blood sample to confirm the

pregnancy if you wish. Do you want to keep the baby?'

Sofia shook her head, her eyes welling up with tears. 'I don't know. My father will be furious.'

'You live with your father? What about your mother?'

'She died when I was young.'

Oh. Krystiana knew a little of that pain. She had been left with no parents at a young age, whereas this young girl still had her father.

'You have time to make a decision. You have options. You could keep the baby, or have it adopted. And of course you can also have an abortion. But *you* must be the one to make the decision—no one else can make it for you and no one can force you to make it. Do you understand?'

'Yes.'

'But, again, that's *your* decision.'

Sofia nodded. 'So what do I do now?'

'You think. The first trimester can sometimes be difficult, and not all pregnancies make it through. Take some time to think what you would like to do, and in the meantime I'll book you in with a midwife for a visit. If you'd like to tell your father in a safe environment then you can always do so here, with a member of staff or myself attending. Are you feeling sick at all?'

'A bit.'

'Try nibbling on something as often as you can. Hunger can trigger nausea. Have a biscuit or two at the side of your bed for first thing in the morning, before you get up. Nothing chocolatey—something plain. A ginger biscuit, or something like that.'

Sofia stood up. 'Thank you. You've been very understanding.'

'It's my job.'

When Sofia had left the room Krystiana sat for a moment and pondered her young patient. She had a difficult time ahead of her—a future that no one could predict just yet. And she felt in a similar situation, with her home in disarray. Her living area open to the stars.

She realised that she had always struggled in every area of her life. It was a state of affairs that she had become used to. Perhaps that was why the richness and opulence of the palace made her so uncomfortable? It hid the real world. It wasn't reality. It was a mirage.

Krystiana liked her minimalism. Her stone. Wood. Brick. She wasn't used to marble and crystal and silk. She wasn't used to servants and having things done for her. She enjoyed the simplicity of making her own breakfast. Chopping up fruit and adding it to a bowl of oats gave her pleasure. She liked looking after her own home. Polishing it. Sweeping the floors, cleaning her bathroom.

At the palace those sorts of chores were done by servants. And she didn't like the idea that someone else was having to pick up after her. It didn't feel right. It felt as if parts of her everyday life were being taken from her. And since moving to the island Krystiana had started relying on her gut feelings and instincts, because she'd realised rather swiftly that they were the only things she could trust.

She reached for the phone, intending to dial the palace and tell them not to send her a car because she was going to make her own way. But then she realised she didn't know the number, and that all her things—her clothes, her personal computer, everything she valued—were there. She had to go back. Maybe just for one more night? And then she would pack her things.

She wasn't Matteo's doctor any more. He didn't need her. She'd told him about their shared experience and she didn't need to share any more. Because she knew that if she did stay his friendship, his easy nature, would cause her to share more. But she couldn't do that. Because sharing with him would mean *trusting* him.

And she couldn't trust anyone ever again.

Visiting the building site that was Krystiana's home, Matteo had felt incredibly disturbed. One half of the villa looked fine, the other a total wreck. They had picked their way through the rubble, being careful not to stumble, and then Krystiana had found her mother's photograph.

Watching Krystiana crumble like that had opened his own scars. They had both lost their mothers. They both knew that kind of loss. His heart had gone out to her and before he'd been able to stop himself he had pulled her into his arms and held her tight.

He had wanted to make her feel better—wanted to let her know that she wasn't alone. That was all. But listening to her cry, feeling the wetness of her tears seeping through his shirt, he hadn't wanted to let her go.

Realising that had disturbed him. What was he doing? Getting involved in her life like this? Inviting her to stay? Offering to rebuild her home? Sheltering her not only with his house but with his arms, his embrace? He didn't need to be worrying about someone else like this. He did *not* need another emotional crisis in his life. He'd had more than enough to last a lifetime! Getting involved with others, caring for them, only caused him pain in the long run.

And then she'd stepped away from his arms and he'd felt relief. Relief that she was trying to be strong all by herself. It was a clear sign that she did not want to depend upon him and that was fine by him. He didn't need anyone depending upon him personally like that. He knew he could never give anyone what they'd want from him. He'd vowed never to love again, so if he couldn't care for someone like that what was the point? He'd been humiliated once.

He'd felt some of the pressure he'd been putting on himself dissipate. But of course then he'd felt guilty for acting so selfishly. Princes were not meant to be selfish. They were not meant to look out only for themselves, but to look out for their people. And wasn't Krystiana one of his people?

After the car had dropped her off at work he had returned to the palace to carry out his duties. He'd had a pile of reports that needed to be read and signed off, and he'd also needed to meet with his secretary to discuss his schedule for the next few months.

He had a busy time coming up. His father, the King, was going to abdicate within the year—on his seventieth birthday. These next few months would be a whirlwind of appointments, visits, public walkabouts and royal duties. Everybody wanted to see the man who would soon be King.

But as he'd sat at his desk he hadn't been able to concentrate. All he'd been able to think about was Krystiana. How displaced she was. The disruption in her life and what he could do to make it better.

He'd ended up pacing the floors and constantly checking his watch. She'd finish at six p.m. and then the car would bring her home.

He knew he needed to sort his head. Clear it. He knew he needed to create more distance between them. He couldn't let her in past his defences. The risk simply wasn't worth it.

He'd already lost his mother, his wife, and almost his child. That was too much loss for one person to deal with. Letting someone in, letting them get close, was dangerous. Matters of the heart were terrifying in how vulnerable they could make a man. They were a weakness. One that those guerrillas had used with impunity, making him think that his wife and child had been killed.

He would let Sergio deal with Krystiana from now on. He didn't think she would be upset by that. Hadn't she been the one to push him away in the villa?

He was only doing what they both wanted.

So why did he feel disturbed by it?

Krystiana came back to the palace after work and hoped that she would be able to get to her quarters without being seen. If she did meet Matteo she would be politeness personified, but she would tell him that she was tired, that she needed to take a shower or a long bath and then she would be going to bed. It was best all round if she left him to get on with being the future King and she got on with being a doctor. She'd helped him out for one day—that was all. She had told him about her past and that was it. It didn't need to go any further than that.

He was a very nice man—kind, considerate and clearly compassionate. Plus, he had the warmest blue eyes she had ever seen. The type of eyes, framed in dark lashes, that invited confidences. She knew without a shadow of a doubt that if she spent any more time in his company, as his friend, she would grow attached to a man who couldn't possibly remain in her life. They were on two separate paths.

He was Crown Prince. She was a medic. And those two things did not have any future unity.

Krystiana hurried to her quarters, closing the doors behind her and walking straight over to her bed. Sitting down on the mattress, she pulled her mother's photograph from her bag, dusted it off with her fingers and placed it on the bedside cabinet, staring at it for a brief moment.

If only you could see me now, she thought. *Living in a palace in Italy.*

It was far removed from where they had lived in Kraków. What would her mother say?

He's handsome. Is he single?

She smiled at her mother's imagined voice

and, raising her fingers to her lips, kissed them and pressed her fingertips to her mother's photo. *'Tęsknię za toba,'* she said. *I miss you.*

A knock at the door had her wiping her eyes and sniffing before she called out 'Come in!'

Sergio walked into the room. 'Good evening, Dr Szenac. His Majesty King Alberto has invited you to join him and his family for this evening's meal.'

'Oh, that's very nice of him but I'm rather tired. It's been a stressful day and I'd really like to just turn in— maybe have a tray brought to my room, if that's okay?'

Sergio nodded. 'I understand.' He turned and made to go, but then stopped, as if changing his mind. 'It would not be wise to turn down the King's invitation, Dr Szenac. I believe this very morning he approved the finance for the renovation of your villa and he wishes to meet with you. I fear he would not take kindly if you did not come.'

Of course. It wasn't just Matteo paying to fix her home. It was coming out of the royal family's purse. To live in their home, to take their money and then not even show her face at dinner would be incredibly rude.

She glanced down at Bruno, who had settled into his doggie bed and was chewing on his toy.

'Right. I understand. Please tell the King that

I will be happy to join him and his family at dinner. What time should I be ready?'

'Dinner is at seven.'

'Perfect. Thank you.'

'The dress code is smart casual.'

She wasn't worried about the dress code. She was worried that they would sit her opposite Matteo and she would end up looking into those deep blue eyes of his all evening.

He didn't always eat dinner with his father. They both led such busy lives, on such different schedules, it was rare for both of them to be home at the same time. But his father had just come back from a short break in Africa and wanted to catch up with his son before a tour around Europe took him away again.

It was a good thing they both enjoyed travelling and meeting new people.

'It was a great shame to be informed about Dr Bonetti's wife. I hear that she has pulled through?' his father asked.

'Yes. My advisor tells me that earlier today she was moved off the critical care unit and on to a ward.'

'That's excellent. I must send them a token of my affection. Remind me to tell my secretary.'

Matteo smiled. 'I will.'

And that was when the doors to the dining room were opened by Sergio.

'Ah! This must be our new guest. Dr Szenac!' The King got to his feet. 'Welcome! I'm so pleased to meet you, though it is such a shame it has to be under such difficult circumstances. How is your home looking?'

Matteo watched his father greet Krystiana, kissing both her cheeks and smiling broadly. Krystiana looked tired, but her eyes were sparkling still.

She curtsied. 'Your Majesty. Thank you. The work has begun, so hopefully I won't have to impose upon you and your family for too long.'

'Nonsense! Our home is your home. We wouldn't have it any other way. Please—take a seat.'

Sergio held out a chair for her and she settled into it—directly opposite Matteo.

He smiled at her. 'How was work today?'

'Interesting. Though it always is. You never know who's going to walk through the door.'

'Keeps you on your toes!' his father said.

She nodded.

Sergio filled her glass with water and laid a napkin over her lap. 'Can I get you a drink, Dr Szenac?'

'I'm fine, thank you, Sergio.'

'We must introduce you to everyone. You know who I am, and my son, but on your right is my sister Beatrice, and opposite her is her husband Edoardo. They're here on a flying visit from Florence.'

Krystiana smiled at them both. 'I'm very pleased to meet you.'

Matteo could see that she was nervous. Surrounded by royalty. Hemmed in by titles. A king, a prince, a duke and a duchess. She was blushing, her face suffused with a rich pink colour in both cheeks, as she struggled to make eye contact with anyone. He hated seeing her looking so uncomfortable.

Knowing how badly her day had started, he decided to rescue her. 'How's Bruno doing with the change in his home-life?'

She looked up at him, grateful. 'He's adapting very well. Almost as if he always suspected he was meant for palace life. I think he likes having servants.'

He laughed, enjoying her smile.

'And how are *you* adapting to being back in palace life, Matteo?' asked his Aunt Beatrice. 'It must be such a relief for you to get back to normal?'

He nodded. 'It is, but I expected it to be different…getting home.'

'How do you mean?'

Beatrice looked extremely interested, but then again she would be. He hadn't seen her since before his kidnapping, and he hadn't had much chance to talk to his father's side of the family about what had happened.

'When you're in that situation, held captive, what keeps you going is the thought of returning home. Of getting back. Of everything being all right again.'

'But…?'

'But it's not that way at all. You feel like you've been held captive in time, and that although everyone else has moved on you're still in the same place. You want to process what has happened, but it's difficult.'

'Your father tells me you had some *therapy* afterwards?' She said it as if therapy was a bad word.

'Yes.' He looked at Krystiana and smiled. She would know what that meant. 'I still am.'

'Really?'

'I've found it to be helpful.'

Beatrice raised a perfectly drawn-on eyebrow, but didn't ask any more.

He shared a look with Krystiana. 'There are some…after-effects you don't expect.'

'Like what?' asked Edoardo, sitting back as the first course arrived and the servants laid steaming bowls of soup in front of them all.

'Bad dreams. And being enclosed in any small

space is a little unnerving now. Being afraid of the dark.'

Krystiana looked up at him. He knew. Knew that she was the same. That she had the same fear as him. And suddenly he didn't want to be at this dinner any more, surrounded by the others. He wanted to be somewhere talking to *her*. Asking her about how she dealt with the same things. Whether she'd beat the fears or still struggled with them.

'And, of course, there was all that business with Mara,' said Beatrice, with a snide tone to her voice. 'I always said she wasn't the one for you.'

Yes, well... 'She was my best friend, Aunt Bee.'

'So she should have waited for you.'

'She was alone and afraid.'

He tried to stand up for his ex-wife, despite his feelings. He knew what she'd gone through. They'd talked about it many times, and as far as he could see she'd done what any person would. The humiliation he'd felt, expecting to come home to a wife when in fact she was actually his ex-wife, had been his to work through.

His aunt sniffed and dabbed at her lips with her napkin. 'Well, so were *you*, I'd imagine.'

'She had no idea if I was alive or dead. She

was trying to raise a baby, all alone, and she was grief-stricken and needed comfort.'

'So she turned to Philippe? An old boyfriend?'

'He was there for her when I couldn't be. Come on, Aunt Bee. You know Mara and I weren't a true love-match. We had an arranged marriage. I would never have stood in the way of her finding her true love.'

'She'd just had your *child*!' Beatrice was clearly appalled by Mara's behaviour.

'That's enough, Bee,' said his father, bringing order to the table. 'I do apologise, Dr Szenac. We are a passionate family and often our get-togethers can be a little…heated.'

She smiled at him. 'That's all right. Please don't apologise. I'm sure it's the same in any family.'

'I'm grateful for your understanding. Is your family like this?'

Matteo saw her take a sip of soup, her hand trembling, and knew it would be difficult for her to answer. Her mother was dead. Her father was in prison.

'I have only my Aunt Carolina, and though we love each other very much we do have our moments.'

His father guffawed. 'So we are normal, then?'

Krystiana laughed, too. 'Yes, you are.'

Edoardo leaned over. 'You're a doctor, I believe?'

'Yes. I have a practice in Ventura, which I share with the royal physician, Dr Bonetti.'

'Ah, yes. I think someone told me that earlier... before you came. Are you married, Doctor?'

She blushed. 'No.'

'Planning on it?'

She shook her head. 'No.'

'Why ever not?' interrupted Beatrice.

Krystiana looked uncomfortable. Again. Matteo understood that his family could be a bit much. They were inherently nosy and thought they were the authority on most subjects.

He interjected for her. 'Marriage isn't the be-all and end-all of life, Aunt Bee. Plenty of people remain happily single.'

'But what's the point of *being* here, then?'

Krystiana looked at him in a panic. 'How did you and Mara meet?' she asked, clearly wanting to divert the topic of conversation away from herself.

'We were distant cousins and we had known each other since we were children.'

'You grew up together?'

He nodded. 'Her father is an earl. We were best friends. Went to school together. I loved hanging out with Mara—it seemed the most obvious thing that we should marry, and of course it strengthened the relationship between our families.'

'You had a happy marriage?'

Matteo shrugged. 'It seemed to be. We had our ups and downs, but all couples do. Our friendship was something that neither of us wanted to lose. And we haven't—despite what happened.' He flicked a look at his aunt, who clearly still disapproved.

'You weren't worried that marriage to one another would change your friendship?' Krystiana persisted.

'No. We knew we loved one another and had done for years. We didn't expect marriage to change that.'

She nodded. 'That's good. I'm glad you were happy together.'

He smiled, feeling they were in some kind of a conspiracy together. 'Me too.'

'And then you had a child together,' added Beatrice, raising her eyebrows as if she doubted the wisdom of that decision.

'Alexandra. She's beautiful, by the way, and I can't wait for you to meet her.' He directed his answer to Krystiana.

'I look forward to it.'

His face was stretching into a broad grin as he looked at her, and he was almost forgetting there were other people around the table. When he did remember, he looked at them to see they were looking at him rather strangely. He looked away and sipped at his wine.

He could remember the look on Mara's face when she'd told him that she was pregnant. She'd looked so happy! And he'd been thrilled too that he was about to be a father. But he'd known Mara wasn't the soul mate he'd always hoped for. Mara had always talked about having children, and about how she hoped to be a good mother to her baby. How she hoped to care for it herself as much as she could, and not let royal nannies get in the way and take over. They'd both had such dreams for their child, and it was disappointing that it hadn't worked out.

But he was pleased for Mara and the happiness that she had found with Philippe. He was pleased that, despite the kidnapping trauma, she had managed to move on with her life and find true joy with a man she loved. A proper love. Romantic love. Something he'd once yearned for but had now vowed to stay away from.

He'd been hurt by what had happened between him and Mara. But he couldn't imagine being in love with someone and losing them, the way his father had lost his mother, the love of his life.

If anything, he was a little envious of Mara. But he knew he wouldn't find anything like that for himself.

Couldn't find that for himself.

Because what if he lost it all again? It had hurt to let Mara go. To let another man help raise his child. And he'd seen the devastation romantic loss could cause.

He didn't ever want to go through that pain. He'd had enough pain already.

Krystiana asked to be excused at the end of the meal, as she had a long day at the practice tomorrow, and Matteo offered to walk her back to her quarters. She was a little anxious about that, but figured it was only a short distance and she could hardly refuse him in front of his family.

And as they walked Matteo began to tell her more about his kidnapping.

'…and then they just came out of nowhere.'

'The people who took you?'

He nodded, those blue eyes of his now stormy and dark.

'Yes. They emerged from the side of the road, holding machine guns and wearing masks. I had to stop the car. Mara was in the back, pregnant, breathing heavily from her contractions.'

'I remember she was in labour. It was on the news.'

'They approached, threatened my men with guns to their heads and pulled me from the vehicle, binding my hands with rope and pulling a dark bag over my face.'

'You must have been terrified!'

'I was. I thought they might do something to Mara, too. That we might lose the baby. I remember struggling, trying to free myself, trying to do what I could to distract them from my wife and unborn child.'

'But they left Mara behind?'

'Yes. They were just after me. I was hit over the head with something. A rifle butt—maybe something else. I think I passed out and they dragged me to another vehicle.'

She shook her head in amazement. 'I don't know how I would have coped with that.'

'We drove for a long time. I tried to remember which way the vehicle turned—right or left— whether I could hear anything outside that might help—like trains or traffic, the sea…anything!'

'And did you?'

'No. We headed deep into the country and I was dragged into somewhere dark and cold.'

'The cave?'

'Yes. I was chained like an animal to a metal post and kept there, underground, for two years.'

Krystiana swallowed hard as they arrived at the door to her quarters. She was imagining it all too clearly. How it must have felt. The panic inside him. The loss of control. The helplessness.

Being at someone else's mercy. She knew how that felt *exactly*.

'Two years… I thought six weeks was a long time.'

'You were just a child.'

'I know, but…'

He looked down at the floor. 'It makes you realise the resilience of the human spirit, doesn't it?'

She nodded, biting her lip. His story reminded her so much of her own, and she'd never had anyone who had been through something similar to talk to about this. The need to share with him was intense.

And that was exactly why she had to go into her room. She'd thought she'd said goodbye to all these memories. Had put all the pain in a box and stored it right at the back of her brain, where it couldn't hurt her any more. But being with him, listening to him talk about his own experiences, made her want to bring it back out again and pick over it. Analyse it. Try to make sense of it.

'Well, I have a long day of work tomorrow. I need to be up, bright and early.'

'Of course.' He nodded, then looked at her. 'How do you sleep?'

She looked into his eyes then, and knew she couldn't lie to him. 'With a night-light. You?'

He smiled, but it was filled with sadness and empathy. 'The same.'

Krystiana nodded. She should have known. She'd always been embarrassed about having one, and she'd never dreamt she would ever tell anyone about it—because why would she need to? No one would ever get that close. But telling him had been easy. *Easy.*

'Well, goodnight, Matteo. I hope you have pleasant dreams.'

'You too, Krystiana. You too.'

She woke early, disturbed by a dream in which she'd found herself back in that bunker, back in that hole in the ground, screaming for someone to find her, to save her, when suddenly the roof had opened. She'd shielded her eyes from the light as she saw someone kneel down and offer her a hand. When she took it, and when she was pulled from the earth, it was into Matteo's arms, and suddenly she'd found herself against his chest.

She'd woken with a start, her heart pounding.

Needing some fresh air before work, Krystiana stepped out into the morning sun and stopped in the gardens for a moment, just to breathe in the warm summer air, her eyes closed.

She'd expected to be alone. No one else awake but the servants, busily working away behind the scenes, but she suddenly felt a presence by her side.

She opened her eyes and saw Matteo. 'Morning.'

'Good morning. Couldn't sleep?'

She couldn't tell him about her dream. 'I just needed some fresh air. I've never enjoyed being cooped up inside.'

He looked out over the gardens. 'No. Nor me. Come on—let me show you everything.'

He walked her down a path that lay before her like something in an exquisite painting. Green hues of olive and emerald, fern and lime, pine and sage, were layered and interspersed with shots of fuchsia, gold, white and rose. Someone talented had landscaped these gardens, and as they walked past lily ponds and bubbling water features, fountains and grottos, she marvelled at all that she could see.

'This is a beautiful place. Are these gardens open to the public?'

'No. They're my own private project.'

She looked at him, amazed. '*You* designed them?'

He smiled. 'Designed them, helped build them, planted almost every seed.'

'But this is *years* of work!'

'I started young. I always had—what do they call it?—green fingers!'

She laughed. 'Yes! Wow. I had no idea. You must have missed it incredibly when you weren't here.'

'I knew they were in good hands. And the thought of them kept me going when I was captive.'

'The memory?'

'I kept imagining myself walking along the paths, lifting a flower to smell its scent. I tried to remember how I'd built it. Created it. In my head I lost myself here many times. But by losing myself here, I *kept* myself. If that makes any sense?'

She nodded. 'It does. It anchored you.'

'*Si.*'

He led her down a curving stepped path, bordered with bushes she couldn't name that were higher than her head, flowering with tiny blue and white flowers, until they emerged in a sun garden that had a sundial at its centre. The floor had been laid with coloured stones—a mosaic depicting a knight fending off a giant green dragon.

'You did this, too?'

'It came from a book I read as a child. The tale of St George and the Dragon. A story that fascinated me. This mosaic was a birthday gift from my mother when I was ten years old.'

'A whole mosaic? My mother used to buy me socks for *my* birthday.'

He smiled. 'Socks are useful. Was it cold in Poland?'

'Only in winter.'

'Was your birthday in the winter months?'

She laughed. 'No. July.'

She went over to look more closely at the sundial. It was made of a dark stone, slate in colour. But marbled with white. She had no idea what it actually was, but the dial itself was exquisite, with a hand casting a shadow to one side.

She checked her watch. 'It tells the correct time.'

'Of course.'

She looked around them, saw that the palace was hidden by trees and bushes. 'You could almost imagine the palace isn't there,' she said.

Matteo smiled.

'If I lived here permanently I'd want a reminder of this at all times of the year, so that even in winter I'd know that spring was coming,' she said.

'Don't you know that anyway?'

'Yes, but...sometimes it takes a long time to get what you want. I'd want to capture this. This beauty.'

'You could take a photograph.'

She looked at him then. 'You know what? I can think of something better!'

He frowned. 'What is it?'

She smiled. 'Just you wait!'

'You want me to *paint*?' Matteo looked at Krystiana, doubtful.

He could plant a flowerbed, landscape a garden, and would eventually rule a kingdom, but to paint a picture? With his fingers? He wasn't a child…

But something about Krystiana's smile made him willing to give it a go. There was something about her. Something compelling. But for the life of him he couldn't work out what it was.

She was lit up from the inside at the thought of painting, and she'd had a servant at the palace fetch her painting equipment from her room. There were easels and palettes, and paints in acrylic and watercolour in all the colours of the rainbow.

'Remind me again why we're not using brushes?'

'Because this is much more fun. Touch the canvas as you create. Be at one with your picture. I want you to paint the garden. Not just what you see, but what it makes you *feel* as you look at it. I want you to try and use colour to feed your emotions into the work.'

'How do I do *that*?'

'Don't think about it too much. Go by instinct—it's what I do.'

He looked at the blank white canvas. 'I feel ridiculous.'

'Forget I'm here.'

'Are you going to be watching me?'

'No, I've got to go to work. But I would love to see your painting when I get back.'

He looked at her doubtfully, but then he closed his eyes for a moment, enjoying the soft breeze over his face, the warmth of the sun upon his skin, and tried to think about how this garden made him feel.

Before he knew it the soft, warm, fragrant breeze of the garden had awakened his senses. And he began.

Krystiana watched him for a moment, mesmerised by the tentative smile appearing on Matteo's handsome face, and when she realised that she was watching *him* more than she was watching the painting, she quietly slipped away.

CHAPTER FOUR

PRINCESS ALEXANDRA ROMANO was a dainty little thing and cute as a button. With her father's features, she had the cutest large blue eyes, framed by thick, long, dark eyelashes and the sweetest smile.

Her father carried her on his hip. 'Alex—meet Krystiana.'

Krystiana gave her a little wave. 'Hello, Alex. You didn't have to meet me from work, Matteo. I'm sure you have plenty of other things to be doing.'

'We were out for a walk. I saw the car pull up and thought I'd introduce you two.'

Behind her, Bruno jumped out of the car and Alex squealed with delight. 'Doggy!'

Matteo put her down so that she could give Bruno a cuddle. He happily rolled over onto his back, tongue lolling.

'I can't compete with a dog!'

'Can any of us?' She smiled at him, then reached into the back seat to grab her bag.

'How was work today?'

'Good. You?'

'Good. I finished my painting, by the way. I'm not sure you'll think it's Picasso, but…it's done.'

'Maybe you could show me later?'

He nodded. 'Sure. Alex? Come on, now, sweetheart. We must go.'

'But I want to play with the puppy!'

Krystiana smiled at her. 'I'm sure Bruno would love it if Alex took him into the garden. I've got some bags if he misbehaves.' She pulled from her handbag a small pouch filled with blue plastic bags.

Matteo took it. 'Thanks. Maybe you could join us later? Collect Bruno before my darling daughter wears him out completely.'

'Sure. I've got some work to do on my computer first.'

'Okay. I'll see you later.'

She nodded, anxious to be away. She'd spent the day worrying about their time in the garden that morning. About how pulled towards him she often felt. Was she a moth? Or was she the flame? Either way, allowing herself to get close to Matteo was dangerous. He was a very attractive man and he was far too easy to talk to, far too easy to care about.

She knew she would fall deeply if she allowed herself. It was a fatal flaw. She was too trusting. And she simply couldn't allow that. She wanted to love and be loved, but she was scared of it. All the people that she had loved had been lost. And the one person who should have loved her the most had hurt her irreparably.

Love did something to people. It twisted them in ways they did not expect and there was no guaranteeing who it might happen to. She didn't want to take any risks with her heart.

'I'll see you later.' He picked up Bruno's lead, and with his daughter began walking the dog away from her.

And that's how easy it is, she thought. *For you to be discarded. For people to move on and leave you behind.*

Her father had loved her so much he had tried to hide her underground, but now that he was in prison did he ever try to contact her?

No.

Some love! And that from the man who should have loved her the most.

Krystiana did not need to be loved so little or so much that someone wanted to ensnare her. Or lie to her, convincing themselves that what she didn't know wouldn't hurt her. Because they'd be wrong.

A relationship with an aunt and a dog was as

far as she would go. Matteo could be a friend, an acquaintance, and nothing more.

Matteo stood watching his daughter play in her sandbox outside. She had such joy in her face as she scooped sand, trying to make herself a sand-castle and then arranging her carved wooden dinosaurs into position, as if they were protecting it.

Alex made all her own sound effects, too. 'Grr…' she said, and made roaring noises as she stomped them around the base of the castle.

He couldn't help but feel his heart swell with his love for her. She was just so perfect. He and Mara might not have been perfect, but their little girl was. As long as she was in his life, then nothing else mattered. She was all he needed and his whole heart was hers. There would never be anyone else and that was okay. She was the most honest person he knew. An open book. He didn't have to worry about Alex breaking his heart. At least, he hoped not.

He knelt down, suddenly feeling the need to be close to her. He smiled—because how could he not when he was with his beautiful daughter?

'Are you building a castle? Or a palace?

'A palace.'

'Ah, I see. Like this one?'

Matteo settled down onto his knees and continued to watch his daughter play. He was so proud of her. Of the way she'd grown so big and strong without his help or influence in her early years. He was so sad that he'd missed them, but he knew that Mara had not let their daughter forget him. His ex and her new love had raised Alex wonderfully. And even though Mara had left him, she'd never taken away his daughter.

Alberto, his father, wouldn't have stood and watched idly as Mara took away the future heir to the throne. And it saddened him that his own mother hadn't lived long enough to see her grandchild grow up. An undiagnosed brain aneurysm had ruptured one evening after she had gone to bed.

'She looks like you when she concentrates.'

He jumped at the voice and stood up, noticing Krystiana holding on to Bruno's lead.

'Krystiana. I thought you were still working?'

'I needed some fresh air. Being inside for a few hours always makes me feel this way. It's so beautiful out here, I'm amazed you ever go back indoors.'

He nodded. 'If I could spend my life out here then I would be a very happy man.'

Kneeling again, he began to build his own sandcastle and situated the dinosaurs around it. He created a small moat and made one of the dinosaurs fall into it. He made an 'ahh...' noise as it fell.

Alex chuckled.

He and Krystiana shared a smile and he felt something inside him—a warmth he hadn't felt before, something weird that made his heart pound—and he had to look away from her, focus on what was happening with Alex.

But he was totally aware of the very second that Krystiana left with Bruno. He momentarily stopped what he was doing and watched her go...

He knew it was late, but she was needed. *Now.*

Matteo banged on her door. 'Krystiana! Are you awake?'

There were some muffled sounds and then he heard her call out.

'I'm coming—hang on!'

He waited, aware of the clock ticking onwards and trying his best not to be impatient. When she finally opened the door he tried not to notice her delightful bed-head and sleepy blue eyes. Nor the fact that she wore a short white robe, tied at her waist, revealing very bare, shapely legs.

'A boat has sunk just off the coast, carrying Syrian refugees. There were families on board. Children. A team has been assembled on the beach, and a rescue operation is underway, but as one of the few medics on the island—'

He didn't need to say any more. The tiredness was instantly gone from her face and instead it was filled with a determination.

'Give me two minutes!'

She ran barefoot across her quarters to the bedroom and yanked open the wardrobe, grabbing a pair of jeans, a soft tee shirt and a jacket, and pulled everything on over her pyjamas. At the bottom of her wardrobe, was a bag that she grabbed, and in much less than the two minutes she'd asked for she was ready to go.

'What do you know so far?'

The royal car raced the team of helpers down towards the beach, where an impromptu camp had been set up to appraise and assess the refugees as they were rescued and brought to shore.

Overhead lights had already been erected, lighting up the coastline, revealing the massive operation already at work. To one side was a tent with a white flag with a red cross on it, and it was to this that she raced.

Matteo had leapt out of the vehicle when they'd arrived and headed straight across the sand towards a small motorised boat that was waiting to take him out to assist with the rescue. It was such a small island, but she was aware that the royal family had helped out in a crisis before. It made them more beloved of their people, showing that they didn't just sit behind the protective walls of their palace but that they got their hands dirty and helped out whenever there was a problem.

Years ago there'd been a small earthquake in Italy, but the tremors and aftershocks had affected Isla Tamoura, bringing down buildings and trapping people in the rubble. Alberto and his son had gone to help there—she could remember seeing it on the news.

She had to assume he knew what he was doing now and that he was in safe hands. Right now she had patients who were wet and cold and in danger of hypothermia.

Krystiana entered the tent and was thrilled to see Dr Bonetti already there, assessing a bedraggled patient. Giving him a quick nod of greeting, she got to work to check on patients of her own.

A woman sat in front of her, huddled in a blanket, shivering. Her eyes were wide and terrified.

She gave the woman a reassuring smile and showed her the stethoscope. 'I'm a doctor. Krystiana. What's your name?'

'R-Roshan.'

'Roshan? I need to listen to your heartbeat, okay?' She patted at her own chest and her patient nodded.

Her chest sounded fine. Her heart-rate was a little fast, but she put that down to the situation. Slowly she tried to communicate with Roshan, explain the examinations she needed to carry out. Blood pressure. Temperature. Pulse. Oxygen saturations. She moved more slowly than she would have liked, but it was important not to frighten this woman any more than she already was.

Her body had been under huge amounts of stress, but all she found was that Roshan was soaked through, a little dehydrated and also very hungry.

As the examination went on Roshan began to cry, saying things in Arabic that Krystiana didn't understand. She seemed to be asking her about something. Pleading. Her words were a cacophony of sounds. What could it be?

Krystiana could only imagine how scared she was. So far away from her home. A place she'd had to flee from for whatever reason. Was her life in danger? What had she offered the captain of the boat in exchange for her passage? Had she given him everything she had? All her money?

It made her sick to think about it.

She gave Roshan an extra blanket, and was just about to check on another patient when Matteo came barging through the tent entrance, a soaked child in his arms.

Roshan cried out and threw off her blanket. *'Qamar!'* she screamed.

Krystiana pointed at an empty cot. 'Over here.'

She watched as Matteo carried the child over and carefully laid him on the bed.

'He's not gained consciousness since we picked him out of the water but he's breathing. I noticed a lump on the back of his head.'

'Ask Dr Bonetti for warm IV fluids. He'll show you where they are. And fetch some more blankets.'

Matteo raced off to do her bidding whilst she examined Qamar and tried to gain venous access.

He was indeed unconscious, but breathing at a steady rate. The lump on the back of his skull indicated that something had hit him hard, knocking him out, though thankfully she couldn't feel any fracture, or a break to the skin that would need stitching.

She peeled him out of his wet clothes—Roshan helping when she realised what Krystiana was doing—and then covered him with the blankets that Matteo brought over.

'I have the IV.'

'I've inserted a cannula—let's get him hooked up.'

'What can I do to help?' he asked.

'Look after Roshan for me. I think she might be his mother.'

She got in the cannula and started the warm IV running. Then she checked to make sure he had no other visible wounds or any broken bones. She checked his heart-rate and it was steady and sure, but he was thin and bony and she didn't know how strong he was. She'd be happier getting him to a major hospital, where they could give his head a scan to make sure there were no brain bleeds or contusions.

She looked over at Matteo, who was doing his best to communicate with Roshan. His clothes were soaked from carrying Qamar, but he wasn't complaining. She was so grateful to him. For getting involved like this. She could see that he was doing a wonderful job with Roshan, who now sat beside the bed of her son, clutching her prayer beads and dabbing at her eyes with a tissue.

'*Shukraan! Shukraan...*' she said to them both.

Krystiana looked at Matteo. 'What does that mean?'

'I don't know. Perhaps she's saying thank you?'

'Maybe. Are there any more?'

'The boats are going to stay out in the bay for a few more hours, but it looks like we got everybody.'

'How many people in total were on that boat?'

'So far, twelve.'

Twelve people in the water.

Dr Bonetti came over to greet Matteo and thank him for his assistance.

'What's the status of the other patients?'

Dr Bonetti looked grave. 'Mild hypothermia in some cases. A couple are a little malnourished, but that can be easily sorted out over the next few weeks. One had a dislocated shoulder that I've re-sited. We did lose one, though.'

'Who?' Krystiana asked.

'An old man. The coldness of the water was too much for his heart.'

She felt awful at the news. What these people must have gone through—trying to find freedom, doing everything they could, even something that was dangerous, to try and achieve it. What must it have been like for them, travelling on that boat, all huddled together without enough rations to go around?

Had Roshan given up her share of fresh water so that her son would survive the journey? Parents did that, didn't they? Loved their children so much they would gladly give up their own lives if it meant their child survived. That was what they were meant to do, anyway, if the situation arose. She'd like to think she would do the same thing.

'What's going to happen to them?'

'We'll keep them here overnight. Make sure everyone is stable. And then they'll have to be transferred to hospital—'

Matteo frowned. 'They'll have to go on another boat?'

'We have a shuttle boat that can take them. We've used it before—they'll make it there safely.'

Matteo frowned. 'A shuttle boat? I have a ship they could use. It would be larger and more comfortable. Faster, too. I imagine they won't want to spend much time on the water again.'

Krystiana looked up at him. 'That's very kind of you.'

'It's the least I can do. I'm just ashamed it's not more.'

She smiled at him, her gaze dropping to his wet shirt. 'You must be freezing. Here—take a blanket.' She offered him one of the warm blankets from the pile and draped it around his shoulders.

He looked down at her as she did so. 'Thank you.'

Krystiana looked up into his blue eyes and fireworks went off in her belly. Those hypnotic eyes of his...those thick dark eyelashes... His soft, full lips...

Blinking rapidly, she cleared her throat and looked away. 'Well, I must get on. Neuro obs and...stuff.'

Matteo also looked awkward. He nodded. 'Of course. I'll go and make arrangements for the ship to escort these people tomorrow.'

She nodded and turned away, feeling the skin

on her face flaming with a heat that she'd never experienced before, her heart pounding, her mouth dry.

What on earth was happening?

And why did she feel like this?

CHAPTER FIVE

SHE DIDN'T SLEEP much that night when she got back to the palace. Her mind was a whirlpool of thoughts.

I'm attracted to Matteo.

It had to be that. She knew what the first flames of attraction felt like and what she'd felt hadn't been flames but a raging fire, out of control.

There'd been another man once. When she'd been at university. Adamo... She'd studied with him and he'd been nice. They'd gone out on a few dates—dinner, dancing—and he'd had the ability to make her laugh.

She'd begun to think she'd found the one. Something that had started as a slow burn had quickly become a flame. She'd fallen in love with him and, determined to be the one who took control of everything, had asked him to marry her.

And that was when her world had come crashing down around her ears again. Because he'd said no. He couldn't marry her. He was already married! Krystiana, to him, had been nothing but a fling.

It had made her feel used and stupid and ashamed. She had let her attraction to him roar out of control as she'd sought the happiness she felt she deserved, but she'd been a fool!

It had taken weeks for her to sleep again, to think straight again. It had been as if she'd been thrown back in time to when nothing made sense and she'd hated that—because she'd always kept herself safe by controlling everything in her life.

After what had happened with her father—and then Adamo, who had humiliated her—she had vowed to herself never to give her power away again. Never to give her heart to anyone. Because those who had your heart had the power to hurt you and she'd been through enough.

But this thing with Matteo…she didn't feel she had a choice. It felt like something that was happening without her having a hand on the steering wheel. She was in a car and it was careening out of control, down a sheer mountainside, and the brakes weren't working.

How could she stop it?

I could leave. I could rent a place. Nothing is stopping me. And that would be my choice, then, wouldn't it?

That seemed a good idea, and it was still a

good idea after breakfast, when there came a knocking at her door. Hoping and praying that it wasn't Matteo, she opened it to see a woman she didn't know holding the hand of Princess Alex, his daughter.

She beamed a smile at the little girl and crouched down to her level. 'Hello, Alex! What are you doing here?'

'I'm going horse-riding!'

'Horse-riding? That sounds fun. I've never done that—aren't you lucky?'

'One day, darling, Krystiana, you will ride a pony of your own.'

She tried to ignore the voice of her father in her head.

'Could you come? Bruno, too?'

She thought about it. She could. After the hullaballoo of last night's rescue she needed something nice and settling. It was the weekend, she didn't have work today or tomorrow, and she really liked Alex. Perhaps it could be the last thing she did before she packed her things and left?

'All right. But I'm going to leave Bruno here. I'm not sure how he is around horses and I don't want there to be an accident. Is that all right?'

Alex nodded. 'Come on, then! We're going *now*!'

'I'll meet you there. I just need to change.'

Alex and the woman who was clearly her

nanny nodded and headed off, whilst Krystiana checked her wardrobe for the right gear. What did people wear to ride horses? She hoped she'd get a gentle one. She'd hate to be stuck on the back of a galloping horse she couldn't stop...

She'd had enough of that kind of terror already.

Krystiana reached up her hand to stroke the mane of a beautiful grey horse. 'She's gorgeous!'

'Her name is Matilde.'

She jumped, not having expected to hear Matteo's voice. She'd thought it would just be Alex and her nanny. Maybe a groomsman, but no one else.

'Matteo...'

He smiled at her and patted the horse on its neck. 'She's a gentle beast and she will look after you.'

'Good. I'll need that. I haven't ridden before.'

He looked surprised. 'No? Then I'm glad you agreed to come along. Everyone should ride a horse at least once. Horses spark a passion that often consumes.'

Horses weren't the only thing that sparked a passion... She'd lain await all night thinking of him.

'Well, I could hardly turn down a princess,

could I? And give up the opportunity of a lifetime?' She'd always wanted to ride a horse.

He laughed. 'No one can turn her down! Once she turns that smile upon you, you're lost.'

She knew the feeling.

'And the dark horse? Is he yours?'

He smiled. 'Galileo? *Si*. A very proud beast.' He could see the uncertainty in her face. Her anticipation. 'Nervous?'

'Yes. A lot.'

'Do you trust me?'

How could she answer that? To say anything but *yes* would be rude. 'Sure.'

'Don't worry. I'll lead Matilde with a guide rope and Sofia will guide Alex's pony. We're only going for a gentle walk through the orchard. No galloping.'

He smiled to reassure her.

'Alex, *mio cara*, let's get you up in that saddle.' He lifted his daughter up onto the horse's back, making sure she was secure and steady before letting go. 'Your helmet is on tight?'

'*Si*, Papà.'

Krystiana looked uncertain. 'I may need help getting up on this beast. How do you do it without falling off the other side?'

Matteo smiled at her. He held Matilde's reins firmly and showed Krystiana how to put her foot into the stirrup and hoist herself into the saddle.

She did it quickly, not wanting him to have to hold her around the waist or touch her bottom, because if he touched her anywhere below the belt line she feared for her heart-rate.

He mounted his own steed.

'Are we all ready?'

The two women nodded.

'Alexandra?'

His daughter nodded, her eyes on her horse's neck.

He made a small noise of encouragement to his horse and used his stirrups to urge the animal into a walk. The other three followed behind as he led them into the orchard.

The sun shone down on them from above, warming her bare arms and feeling good. As she adjusted to the horse's gait Krystiana found herself relaxing somewhat, beginning to enjoy the adventure.

It was everything she'd hoped it would be. The horse's motion was almost a rocking movement, hypnotic in its rhythm, and with the warmth of the sun and the beautiful orchard all around them she felt herself wanting to just relax and drift off—especially as she'd lost a lot of sleep last night.

It was such a strange world, she thought. That one moment she could be attending refugees on a beach, and the next moment be horse-riding.

What were Roshan and Qamar doing now? And the others? Were they already in hospital? Were they feeling better?

Matteo led the parade of horses down a steep slope and along a small grassy path that would take them into the main thicket of trees.

As they moved along she listened to the birds singing, and then she heard the steady trickle of water and smiled when he led them towards a small babbling brook. Picture-perfect.

They stopped for a moment, and the horses sniffed at the water but chose to nibble on the tall grass alongside it.

'Is everyone all right?' asked Matteo.

Krystiana nodded—as did Sofia, the nanny.

'*Si*, Papà,' said Alex.

He smiled and urged the horses onward.

He'd not known Krystiana would be horse-riding with him and Alex. He'd thought it was just going to be himself, the nanny and his daughter. It had been a surprise to see her standing there at the stables, in figure-hugging jeans and a checked shirt. All she needed was a Stetson and she would look like a proper cowgirl.

Her long hair was in its usual plait. He'd spent the entire night, tossing and turning in bed, wondering what her hair would look like spread out over a pillow.

That moment they'd shared in the refugee tent had been...*electric*. He'd felt it. He'd noticed that she felt it too, but luckily she'd done something to avoid it.

He didn't need the complication of another relationship. He'd married his best friend and hadn't made that work—what hope would there be for anyone else? Plus, he couldn't contemplate the *idea* of another relationship. If you loved someone, you lost them, and the pain of that was too much.

His father was a different man since losing Matteo's mother, and when he himself had come home to find his mother dead and that his wife had moved on and begun a new relationship, he'd decided there and then that the only person he would ever love again would be his daughter.

He wasn't looking for love. Or a fling. His position dictated that a fling would be very bad news indeed. The Crown Prince of Isla Tamoura did *not* use women in such a way. He had standards. And morals.

Any deeper relationship was a no-go, so...

But seeing her here this morning had fired his blood once again, and he was glad that she was a novice with horses—it meant that he could lead without having to look at her or make eye contact, and everyone seemed quite content to just ride along and view the scenery in peace and quiet.

Not that his mind was peaceful. Or quiet. It was coming up with a million and one thoughts about Krystiana that he kept trying to push away.

I am not risking my heart again. No way.

The kidnapping, and then coming home to find his marriage over, his mother dead, were three huge stresses he'd already had to cope with, and there was his coronation coming up at the end of the year…

He just wanted to relax whilst he had the chance. He did not need the added complication of a forbidden crush. Because that was what it would be. They'd shared an experience. They'd both been glad to find someone else who knew how that felt—that was all.

A mind trick. The body playing games.

He knew he was stronger than that. He'd spent two years wondering if this was the day he was going to die and carrying on anyway. If he could get through *that*, then he could get through *this*.

A few more weeks and she'd be gone from his life. Any future physicals would be conducted by Dr Bonetti, and if he retired he would ask another doctor to take over that particular duty.

He could resist his feelings for a few more weeks.

CHAPTER SIX

'She's beautiful…' whispered Mara.

Matteo looked over at his ex-wife, who lay on their daughter's bed as she went off to sleep. 'She is.'

Mara smiled. 'I wasn't talking about Alex. Though she is *very* beautiful, of course. I meant the woman I saw you with.'

He decided to play ignorant. He didn't need his wife playing games. 'You've already met Sofia. You hired her.'

'The *doctor*, Matteo.'

He raised an eyebrow. 'Krystiana? She's just staying here until her place gets fixed.'

'Is that all?'

He picked up the book they'd been reading to Alex and quietly slid it back onto his daughter's bookshelf. 'Of course that's all.'

'Are you sure, Matteo?'

He raised an eyebrow. 'Yes.'

'*Krystiana?* Not Dr Szenac?'

'We're friends. You call friends by their first name. Remember, Mara? We're friends—it's what *we* do.'

She nodded. 'Of course! Of course that's what friends do. I'm just not sure I've ever seen *friends* look at each other the way you two do.'

'I barely know her.'

'You barely know her or you're friends?'

His ex-wife slowly got off the bed, hoping their daughter wouldn't wake. They both crept from the room and Mara pulled the door almost closed as they headed into the next room.

Matteo handed his ex-wife the glass of wine she'd started earlier. 'Please don't, Mara.'

She stared him down. 'Don't what?'

'Don't try to matchmake.'

'I'm not! But I *am* asking you to be careful.'

'You're hinting. Just because you're all loved up, and you feel guilty about giving up on me, it does not mean I'm your responsibility.'

'I'm not trying to fix you up, Matteo. I'm asking you to think carefully about what you're doing.'

He shook his head at her, amused. 'Nothing's happened.'

She smiled. 'Keep it that way—or you're going to hurt a lot of people.'

The next day Krystiana found herself standing outside her villa with Aunt Carolina, who had agreed to meet her there. Some progress had been made. A lot of the loose rubble had been cleared and the first-floor ceiling had been propped up by scaffolding and made secure, whilst a lot of the loose brickwork had been hacked back, so that the hole in her wall had become almost twice the size. Inside, her furniture looked forlorn and strange, open to the elements, but she thanked her lucky stars that there'd been no rain and therefore no water damage.

'Carlo!' She waved to the foreman and he waved back, jumping down from a digger that was removing debris to another part of the site. 'How is everything going?'

'It's going as well as can be expected. My team are working hard and at all hours round the clock.'

'Are we still looking at a few weeks' work?'

'Three…four weeks, maybe. As long as there are no more surprises.'

'You've had surprises?'

He smiled. 'Not yet.' He turned to look at her aunt and she realised she hadn't introduced them. She did so.

'Buongiorno.'

She noticed the interested smile on Carlo's face as he looked at her aunt, and saw that Aunt Carolina was smiling back.

'You're working hard all day, every day? Seven days a week?' Carolina asked.

'*Si.*'

'Perhaps I should bring you and your crew some food? Some drinks?'

'That would be very kind of you—thank you. We lose a lot of time on lunch breaks, going to find food to eat, so that would help us work faster.'

Carolina beamed. 'Well, I'd like to think I was helping...'

Krystiana looked from one to the other and found herself smiling. Who'd have thought it? Carolina and Carlo? Her aunt had lived alone ever since her divorce, years ago, and had always said that men were more trouble than they were worth.

Clearly she was having a change of heart!

'Come on. We need to get going or we'll be late for lunch ourselves.' Krystiana interrupted.

'Of course. I'll see you later, Carlo.'

Carolina waved as she walked away with her niece back to their car.

Once inside, Krystiana turned to her. 'Well, *you've* changed your tune!'

'He was a very nice man!'

'They all are. To begin with. You tell me that all the time.'

'Maybe so—but being alone isn't all it's

cracked up to be. You have to give someone a chance to prove you wrong.'

Did she? Her father had proved her *right*. Those who had your heart could hurt you the most. As Adamo had. Did she have to give Matteo a chance? He seemed nice and kind. He seemed a good, strong, caring man. But what if that was just his public persona? What if he was someone else entirely?

The smile on her aunt's face put doubt into her mind for the next couple of hours, and she found herself wondering, as she was being driven back to the palace, whether she'd been too harsh in her decision-making and ought to give Matteo the opportunity to show her that he was not going to break her heart.

Perhaps if they went out once or twice, and the excitement of something new died down and the fear dissipated somewhat, she'd discover that they didn't have much in common anyway—so what was she worried about?

It could hardly become anything, anyway. He was a prince! He wouldn't enter a relationship lightly, either.

When she got back to her quarters she stared at the suitcase in the bottom of her wardrobe and decided she would leave it there just a little bit longer.

CHAPTER SEVEN

MATTEO HAD INVITED her to dinner in his quarters. He wasn't sure whether he should have or not, but he'd figured, *What the hell?* He was a grown man, they were both adults and they were friends. It wasn't as if he didn't have any self-control. He liked her. He could spend time with her. But that was all it would be.

It wouldn't be a late night. She was bound to be busy, would no doubt have some work to do in her quarters, and he'd only just said goodbye to Mara and Alex, who had gone back to their own private estate in Ventura. There was a load of work for him to catch up on.

He knew he might be playing with fire, but he also knew he couldn't spend the next few weeks jumping out of his skin every time he had to spend time with Krystiana. Best to have a couple of hours in her company and cool the heck down. Okay, so she had beautiful eyes and a nice smile. She was kind and generous and easy to be with…

I'm not exactly talking myself out of this, am I?

He put on some dark trousers and a white shirt. Simple elegance. Something he could feel relaxed in. He didn't want to look as if he was trying to impress her. Because he wasn't. But any gentleman showed respect for the woman he was with by dressing nicely for her.

Krystiana arrived on the dot of seven, her gentle knock at the door signalling her arrival. His heart hammered in his throat and he paused before answering the door, but then he took a deep, steadying breath and swung it open.

And there she stood, looking gorgeous and summery in a blue wraparound dress, that long plait of hers over one shoulder.

'Hi. Come on in!' He stepped back.

'Thanks.' As she stepped in he automatically leaned forward to drop a kiss upon her cheek. He held his breath as he pressed his face close to hers, and his heart almost leapt from his throat as his lips pressed against her skin. She smelt of flowers and soap and something he couldn't quite put his finger on. Whatever it was, it was delicious.

And then he was pulling away and he could breathe again.

She'd flushed a beautiful pink in her cheeks and, clearly trying to distract him from it, she pointed. 'What's that? The painting you promised to show me?'

He nodded at the canvas on the easel, draped with a cover, smiling, but looking apprehensive. 'I'm no Da Vinci, but, yes. Here you go. What do you think?'

He pulled the cover off with a flourish so that she could see it.

An explosion of colour leapt out and he watched her face carefully as she picked up the canvas to consider it properly. Clearly he was new to painting, but he had tried hard and his use of colour was good for an amateur. Even if he said so himself. He'd enjoyed doing it and considered doing so again.

No, he wasn't Da Vinci, or Picasso, or any other famous painter. But it was definitely a Romano. Rich in texture and colour, a riot of green interspersed with cobalt blue, scarlet red and sunshine-yellow. A vast blue sky clear of clouds sat overhead, and he'd even attempted the mosaic floor, using his fingertips for each tile.

'Matteo, it's marvellous!'

'Thank you.' He was pleased that she liked it—he took pleasure from *her* pleasure.

'Are you sure you did this? It's beautiful! You've done a wonderful job for your first time.'

'Imagine what I'd be like with practice.' He smiled.

She looked at him, her smile uncertain.

'Yes! Yes, I imagine you would be brilliant!' She laid the canvas back upon the easel and admired it better by stepping back. 'You've captured the very essence of the garden. Full of life and joy. This will keep you going in the winter months when there's less in bloom.'

And suddenly he knew something. 'I'd like you to have it.'

'Me?'

He nodded. 'I can look at the real thing every day. You'll be going home soon and I'd like to think you will remember your visit.'

It saddened him to think of her leaving. She was a kindred spirit. Someone who had experienced the same thing as he and that was important. Who else would understand what he had gone through?

But it was more than that shared experience. There was a naturalness about Krystiana. Something about her that spoke to him. And it was confusing and worrying and exciting in different ways. But that was the whole point of tonight. To show that he could deal with that and not act on it. Krystiana could never be more than his friend, and that was the thing that he needed to remember more than anything else.

Besides, princes could not be with commoners. It was against the law of his country. So…

that was that. As Mara had tried to forewarn him. And it was a *good* thing, because it kept him safe. She was out of bounds and men like him did not have flings. The media would have a field-day if he did. But thankfully his heart was boxed away. To all intents and purposes it was still in that mountain cave and he had to leave it there.

'I'm honoured. Thank you.'

He smiled, and being caught in her gaze once again was exhilarating. Everything else faded away and all he saw was her. He blinked and stepped back, indicating they should go further out onto the terrace, where the views were impeccable in the late evening light.

'Would you like to take a seat? Sergio will be here momentarily with the first course.'

'What are we having?'

A dash of attraction with a hint of lust and a heavy dose of desire.

'I told him to surprise us. I'm sure he won't let us down. He has quite the palate.'

'Really?'

'His family own a winery. Up in the Auriga Hills.'

Good. That's better. Talk about Sergio. The most unromantic topic you can think of. Wine and grapes and feet squishing grapes in age-old barrels. Sergio's feet. Yes, now, there's an image.

'I didn't know that.'

'I'm sure he'd love to show you around one day.'

'Have you ever been?'

'Yes. A few years ago now, though. Before I was kidnapped.'

She nodded. 'How do you feel about it now?'

He didn't mind talking to her about that, either. 'Sometimes it's like a dream. Like it never really happened to me. Other times it's like a nightmare and I remember everything. How about you?'

'Well, it's been a lot longer for me since it happened. But I understand what you mean. I tried to make sense of it once, by going to the place where it had happened. I thought if I confronted it then it wouldn't have any power over me.'

'What was that like?'

'Strange. The landowner agreed to walk me out to the spot where my father had created the bunker. He was very sweet to me. Very kind. Asking after my well-being, wanting to know that I was all right. He even apologised to me for not knowing. For not realising that I was out there. And then he pointed at a dip in the ground. It just looked so normal and inconsequential. No different from the rest of it. And yet in my mind it had held such power. The hole had been filled in, and scrub and mulch covered it over, but I stared at it, trying to imagine myself in such a small hole, shivering in the cold, clutching a book for comfort.'

He could imagine it all too easily. 'Did you have nightmares before?'

'Every night.'

'And going to the place…did that help get rid of them?'

'It did. I saw it was just a place that meant nothing any more. It wasn't the bunker that had harmed me—it was my father. That takes longer to get over. Someone close hurting you. But, yes, it was a good thing for me to do. It exorcised the ghosts that lingered. Gave me closure.'

'How so?'

She glanced at him. But thankfully not for too long. Her eyes were like welcoming pools he wanted to stay in.

'I think it's because it was the place I wanted to escape from so much. A place I told myself I would never again go near. I'd built it up into this huge thing. So that place…it haunted me. By returning I showed that I was stronger. I proved to myself that *I* was in control.'

Matteo nodded. He understood. And he was in awe of her bravery and courage.

'You could go back too, you know. I believe in you. If you could get through two years in that place, then you can get through anything.'

'I don't have to go back. I've thought about

it, but the bad dreams are only occasional and my therapist has been helping me a lot…sorting through my feelings.'

'Good. Talking therapy works really well. I'm glad you're getting a lot from it.'

He nodded. 'I am.'

At that moment Sergio arrived, carrying a tray, and laid down a small bowl in front of each of them. 'Butternut squash risotto,' he intoned. 'Do enjoy your meal.'

'Do you think being held hostage made you a different person?' she asked after a while.

'I'm still me.'

'Of course—but are you a stronger you now?'

'I'd like to think so. I've been given a different perspective on life. On trauma and struggle and just wanting to survive. I'd like to think I have taken that and learned from it, so that I can be a strong king when I take the throne.'

'You'll make an *excellent* king,' she said emphatically.

He was pleased at her confidence in him. It was something he shared. 'Thank you. I shall certainly try my very best.'

She nodded. 'I've no doubt. What other royal opens up his palace to a homeless woman? Helps search for survivors under earthquake rubble? Goes out to rescue asylum seekers? You're not afraid to get your hands dirty. You care. You're compassionate. You'll make an excellent monarch.'

She clearly meant every word. He was truly touched by her confidence in him. 'Thank you. That means a lot to me.'

She stared back and he found himself caught in her gaze. What *was* it about her that did this to him?

'Eat your risotto before it gets cold.'

She nodded, smiled and picked up her fork.

She imagined, as he spoke, what it might be like to be with him. Who wouldn't? He was a prince. Handsome and charming. A presence with an overwhelming masculinity that made itself known whenever she was with him. He was a good listener, a caring and thoughtful person, and she could see that he liked people.

He was always courteous and considerate to the servants in his employ, chatting to everyone the same way, no matter whether they were another member of the royal family or a gardener. She could appreciate his kindness, his heart, and his concern for his people and the future he might bring them. Clearly being King was something he took seriously.

But her body responded to him in ways she did not want. Her heart fluttered with excitement every time she saw him and she yearned for something more than what they had. But that was just her being foolish. A remnant from a previous time in which she'd trusted people.

'How do you see your life changing when you become King?' she asked, genuinely interested.

He shrugged. 'I imagine it will be pretty much the same. Just my title will be different. I'll be expected to attend more events. To do more touring, perhaps.'

'Isn't it hard for you to be away from your family?'

'It can be. The kidnapping made me see how important family is. Material things—possessions—those don't matter at all. It's people who count. Being with the ones you love. Leaving them hurts me, but it gets easier each time I do so.'

He ate a mouthful of their next course—a rich lasagne, oozing with béchamel sauce.

'What about you? You left your childhood home and moved to another country. Don't you ever miss Poland?'

'Sometimes. But I'm not so sure it's the country I miss as much as the people I knew there. Friends I made at school. The therapist I saw who became a good friend. My school teachers.'

'You enjoyed school?'

She smiled. 'I did. Very much so. I even thought

I'd become a teacher when I was little—I loved it that much.'

'What made you become a doctor?'

'My mother dying the way she did. Hit by a bus. When I got to the hospital and saw how they were trying to save her, I…' Her mouth dried up and she had to take a sip of water. 'I felt in the way. I wanted to help too, but there was nothing I could do but cower in a corner. It wasn't until much later—after I'd moved to Isla Tamoura— that I decided I would never feel that helpless again and so I trained as a doctor.'

'You had focus?'

'Yes. It helped me a lot. Knowing I was work- ing towards something.'

'I feel the same.'

'How so?'

'I grew up knowing I would become King one day. They train you for it, you know. Special les- sons in law and etiquette and the history of tradi- tion. They school you in politics and languages and even body language.'

She laughed. 'Really?'

'Really.' He smiled. 'I've always wanted to be a good king. As good as my father and loved by my people. But I've always known I don't want to be just a title behind the palace walls. I want to be involved—I want to get right down at the grass roots and know people. Be an active king who achieves things and is not just a figurehead. I want to be seen doing worthwhile work, not just waving at crowds from behind bullet-proof glass. Being a man of the people means a lot to me, and I intend to get it right. The kidnapping showed me just how much people matter, and if I can help them then I will.'

'Like housing homeless doctors?'

Matteo smiled. 'Exactly.'

She ate another mouthful of food, contemplating her next question.

'What?' he said.

She looked up at him.

'I can tell you want to ask me something.'

Krystiana dabbed at her mouth with a napkin. Then sipped her water. 'Do you ever get lonely?'

He looked straight back at her, considering her question. 'Do *you*?'

'I asked first.'

Matteo sat back. 'There's an element of being a royal that makes you lonely. People put you on a pedestal—they think you're above them so they don't try to reach you. They just admire you from afar. I'd like to think that I'm accessible to everyone, but... I have my father and my daughter. And my extended family, like Beatrice and Edoardo.'

'That's not what I meant.'

'What *did* you mean?'

'Do you miss being married?'

'My marriage to Mara was never a true love-match. Not romantic love, anyway. We were best friends and we still are, despite what happened. I haven't lost her. What about you? Do you ever see yourself settling down?'

She shook her head. 'No. No way.'

'Why not?'

How to answer? Krystiana looked out across the terrace, past the gardens and deep into the countryside, where the setting sun was making everything look hazy and dark. Should she tell him about Adamo? *No.* That was a whole embarrassing situation she never wanted to be in again.

'I don't think I'm capable of giving myself wholeheartedly to anyone. Not any more.'

'Why not?'

'Because I'd have to trust them, and that would make me vulnerable, and I promised myself I would never be made to feel vulnerable ever again.'

She stared back at him as if daring him to challenge her. To argue with her. Perhaps to laugh at her silly fears.

But he didn't do any of that.

He simply nodded in understanding. 'Okay. Good enough.'

* * *

'Well, thank you for inviting me to dine with you. I've had a wonderful time.'

Matteo nodded. 'It was my pleasure.'

They stood together by the doors, awkwardly trying to work out how to say goodnight to each other.

He felt that the right thing to do would be to kiss her on the cheek as he said goodbye, but when he'd done that earlier he'd inhaled her scent of soap and flowery meadows and felt a surge of hormones flood his system with arousal and attraction. If he did it again he simply wouldn't get to sleep tonight, and he'd already spent enough sleepless nights lately.

'It will be my turn to entertain you next.'

'I'll look forward to it.'

'All right. Well…goodnight, Matteo.'

'Goodnight, Krystiana.'

He hesitated, and reason told him it would be impolite just to walk away, strange to shake her hand and downright rude to do nothing at all. *Friends* kissed each other goodnight—and they were friends, weren't they?

Leaning in, he kissed one cheek, then the other, trying his hardest not to breathe in her delicious scent.

That would be wrong.

For him *and* for her.

It was just attraction. Nothing more. He couldn't be with her. Nor did he want to be. Being with Krystiana would mean falling hard for her and he wouldn't let that happen. He lived his life in the public eye. She'd be scrutinised down to her every blood cell by the press. And hadn't she just told him that she would never be vulnerable again? Nor trust anyone? Plus she'd already said that she didn't want to get into a relationship anyway, so…

Being in the public eye made you vulnerable. Being in a relationship made you vulnerable. It laid you out bare and then fate would tear you to pieces. Life was cruel and impossible to win. He wouldn't even try to put either of them through that.

But he knew he was attracted to her. She was so easy to talk to. He felt relaxed when he was with her. His true self. He could tell her things that he would never tell anyone else…

He shook his head vehemently as he closed his door. Nothing could come of it. No matter how much his body cried out for the intimacy of hers.

He could fight instinct. He could fight attraction.

And what would be the point in getting involved with someone he knew was not suitable? Falling for Krystiana would *destroy* him. He knew it. She was the type of woman he would fall hard for and he didn't want to be laid open to hurt again. Or humiliation when it all went wrong. And why wouldn't it? Everything else had.

Her life was going in one direction and his in another. They were in a fake bubble right now, and it wasn't sustainable.

Matteo turned and walked straight into his bathroom.

He needed a cold shower.

Krystiana smiled at Mara, who sat opposite her in a splendid pure white tailored dress. The dress showed off Mara's sylph-like figure, all long limbs and elegance and grace. They'd met in the corridor of the palace as Mara had dropped off Alex and they'd come for a coffee in the royal gardens.

'What was it like for *you* when Matteo was taken?'

Krystiana was intrigued. She wanted to know what it had been like for those left behind. She was thinking specifically of her own mother, as they'd never had much time to talk about it before she died.

Mara let out a slow sigh. 'It was very difficult. No one knew what had happened to him and I feared the worst. Especially as I'd seen their treatment of him when he was taken. They hit him over the head with a rifle. The sound it made will haunt my dreams for ever.'

'Didn't you have guards? A convoy of any kind?'

'Yes, of course. But they took out the lead car and then surrounded us with armed men. And there'd been a new guard riding with us, who was actually one of them, and he had his gun at Matteo's head. They had no choice but to back down.'

'And then what happened?'

'Then he was gone. I screamed. I cried. I had to get into the front of the car to use the emergency radio. I was still contracting. Still in labour. It seemed an age before help arrived.'

'You gave birth *alone*?' Krystiana could hardly imagine that. At least her mother hadn't seen her being treated roughly. Had never seen inside the hole in the ground. Had not had to go through something like childbirth afterwards.

'My mother came, and my sister. They were able to get to the hospital in time.'

'And it was an easy birth?'

'My blood pressure was high, but the doctors felt that was because of what had happened. The trauma of Matteo's kidnapping. The violence. I delivered in Theatre—just in case it became an emergency and they needed Alex out quick.'

'You must have been frightened?'

'Very.'

'Alex was all right?'

'Yes.' Mara smiled. 'She was beautiful.'

'She still is.' Krystiana smiled too. 'Is Alexandra the name you both chose?'

'It was one of Matteo's choices. I'd not been sure about it, but with him gone like that... I had to choose it. And now I love it. It suits her perfectly.'

'You had no doubt that he'd return?'

'At the beginning? None at all. But when time kept passing. Days into weeks. Weeks into months. A year... I began losing hope. I wanted my child to have her father.'

'That must have been hard for you.'

What had her mother felt as each day passed? Each week? A month? Had she feared her daughter dead?

Mara nodded. 'It was. To lose my best friend, the father of my child... I felt incredibly alone. But I was expected to carry on. Be a representative of the royal family. Appear brave in the face of the *paparazzi*. It became too much, and I began to lean on an old family friend.'

'Philippe?'

She nodded. 'I know a lot of people hate me for it. For moving on. But when you're so alone... your heart cries out for comfort.'

Krystiana considered that. The need to be held

was a powerful one. To be listened to. *Heard.* When was the last time someone had given her a long hug? When had she last snuggled against someone? Bruno didn't count. He was a dog. But perhaps she felt she could do it with Bruno because dogs loved unconditionally? Dogs didn't trick you, or let you down, or bury you in a miserable hole.

And as she gazed at Mara she wondered. Wondered how she could seem so content, so happy, knowing that life could be unfair and take your loved ones away from you so quickly?

'You and Philippe are happy?'

She smiled. Beamed, in fact. 'Very.'

'I'm glad for you. That you found Philippe.'

Mara nodded her thanks.

CHAPTER EIGHT

'*OUCH!*' KRYSTIANA WHIPPED her hand from the rose bush, shaking it madly to take away the pain. One of the thorns must have pricked her as she'd knelt down to smell the scent of the misty blue bloom.

The rose was called Blue Moon. Her favourite. Her mother had grown Blue Moons in her small patch of garden, and as Krystiana had wandered through the gardens that gave Matteo peace she had hoped to find some for herself. Spotting the familiar bloom had drawn her to it, and she had reached for it without thinking.

'Are you all right?'

She spun to see Matteo coming towards her. He looked very handsome today. Dark linen trousers and a white shirt, the sleeves turned up to the elbow.

She glanced at her finger and saw a small drop of blood forming. 'I'm fine. I just caught myself on the thorns.'

'Let me see.'

She shook her head, backing away. 'No, it's all right. I—'

But he had her hand in his, examining it carefully, his touch gentle, yet commanding.

She had to stand there, breathing shallowly, trying not to stare at him as he looked at her hand. She did not want this. Did not *need* this. His proximity. His tenderness in looking out for her.

'Really, it's all right.' She insisted.

'You're bleeding.' He reached into his pocket and withdrew a white handkerchief.

'It'll stain...' She tried to protest, but he wrapped it around her finger anyway. She sagged, feeling him apply pressure. She also winced.

'Does it hurt?'

She shrugged. 'I don't know. Maybe a little.'

'Perhaps you have a thorn in it?' He removed the handkerchief for a closer look, but it was hard to see as blood kept coming.

She really wanted her hand back. Having him being this attentive to her was really playing with her mind.

'I've got tweezers in my bathroom. I'll check later.'

She yanked her hand free from his and gave him a brief smile, trying to appear grateful when in reality, she felt anything but. No. She *was* grateful. But that was just one of the many things she was feeling.

'What are you doing out here? I thought you had a meeting?'

In fact that was the reason she had come out here in the first place. She knew it was his sanctuary, but she'd known he was meant to be busy and she'd needed space to breathe and think.

'It got cancelled.'

'Oh.' She bit her lip, trying to think of something to say. 'You didn't want to go and see Alex instead?'

'She's napping. I'm planning to spend some time with her when she wakes up. I came out to find you because I thought you might like to hear about what happened with Roshan, Qamar and the others.'

She was very interested. 'Oh, yes?'

'They made it safely to the hospital. Qamar regained consciousness quite quickly and his dehydration issues and malnutrition are being thoroughly taken care of by a specialist team of dieticians.'

That was wonderful news. 'I'm glad. What will happen next for them?'

'They'll be found homes, once the doctors give them the okay to leave, and I've put out a few feelers with the authorities to see what we can do—maybe get them some work, places in schools, that kind of thing.'

She smiled. He was so good. So generous. Selfless. She liked that about him. 'That's fantastic. I hope they find the peace that they deserve.'

'Me too.'

'And you? What are you going to do today, now you're free?'

'We're going to go swimming in the pool.'

'Oh, that's nice.'

He smiled. 'Well, I don't get to go to public pools, and I love swimming. Mostly in the sea, but the pool will do. You should come too.'

Krystiana in a pool? In a swimsuit? With Matteo, who'd be wearing nothing but shorts? That was a little too intimate for her liking.

'I…er…think I'll pass.'

'Come with us. It will be fun.'

'Not for me, it won't.' It was out before she could censor it.

He frowned. 'Why not?'

A million excuses ran through her head and she considered them all. But her hatred of lying convinced her to tell him the truth. If he knew, then he would leave it alone and not force the issue.

'I can't swim.'

'What?' He looked at her incredulously.

'I can't swim. I never learned.'

'You had no one to teach you?'

'No.'

She felt her cheeks flush. After her kidnapping she had been too busy with her head stuck in books, and swimming had seemed a luxury that she didn't want to pursue. What would have been the point? She never intended going near water, except to maybe admire it. She never wanted to go in it.

Yes, she now lived on an island, surrounded by water, and after seeing what had happened to those refugees they'd rescued perhaps she ought to, but...

Matteo beamed and his smile melted her heart.

'Then I will teach you.'

'No.'

'Come on. You'll thank me for it.'

'No, I... I don't even have a costume!'

'We'll buy you some.'

'No, honestly, Matteo, it's fine—'

'I won't take no for an answer.'

She could see in his eyes how much he wanted to help her learn to swim. How much he wanted to give something back to her. How excited he was by the idea.

She thought of her pale, pasty body next to his tanned, glowing sun god look and cringed inside. It would be embarrassing, wouldn't it? And spending some downtime with him would only add to the feelings she was already having. She couldn't let that happen.

How on earth am I going to get out of this?

He had to admit to himself that he hadn't quite thought this through—offering to teach Krystiana to swim. He'd just blurted out the invite. It had seemed the right idea at the time and he hadn't been able to get past the knowledge that she didn't know how to. Swimming was something he had always done, and he found a freedom in the water that couldn't be found elsewhere. It was soothing. Good for the mind. And he wanted to share that with her, knowing that she had been through the same kind of trauma as he.

As she entered the pool house, looking nervous, wearing a thin robe, he saw her long, elegant legs and got a flash of intensity through his body. There was something about her. So innocent. So vulnerable. So alone. He could connect with those feelings. He'd felt the need to surround her and protect her this afternoon in the garden, when she'd hurt herself. When he'd seen her bleeding. He'd felt his heart pound and blood rush through his veins.

Okay, it had only been a small puncture wound, but it had been enough to awaken his protective side. He'd wanted to keep the world

out so that he could help her, and then, up close
to her, holding her hand, inhaling the scent of
her, looking into her warm blue eyes it had made
his senses go wild—into overdrive—and he had
not wanted to let go.

When she'd pulled away he'd seen it in her
eyes that she felt something too, and that knowledge had made him stop. She didn't want to get
involved with anyone. Nor did he.

He had to back off. To stay away from her. But
something kept him there. The need to teach her
something. To enjoy the time they had left before their lives reclaimed them. There'd been that
look on her face…one that he couldn't resist…
and then she had told him she couldn't swim. She
lived on an island! And he didn't want her to go
without helping her in some small way.

Getting to the pool before anyone else, he'd
pounded out a couple of lengths already, hoping that by doing so he would exhaust his body
enough not to react to hers. Because he was
aware of just how much he did react to her physi-
cally, and being in the pool would be a lot more
intimate than dinner on the balcony.

He pulled himself from the water and went
over to meet her. 'Hi. Thank you for joining me.'

She looked uncertainly at him, then at the sur-
rounding pool. 'Where's Alex?'

'She'll be here soon. I thought you might appreciate some time one-to-one before she gets here. No one likes to see a five-year-old swim better than them.'

'Oh, that's thoughtful. Thank you.'

'Soon you'll be splashing around like the rest of us.'

'I don't imagine you splash much.'

He smiled and ran his hands over his hair to keep it from his face. 'Maybe not.' He laughed.

'So...' She gazed at the pool, at the way the water rippled, reflecting against the walls and the ceiling. 'How do we make a start?'

He looked at her, feeling his blood surge at the thought and trying to control it. 'You take off the robe.'

She looked at him uncertainly. Hesitant. Torn between wanting to spend this time with him and being afraid of what time with him like this might do.

He was a majestic, gorgeous hunk of man, who seemed oblivious to the effect he was having on her. Which was a good thing—because imagine how embarrassing that might be?

She felt shy about taking off her robe. He might assess her body. Krystiana knew she wasn't considered *unattractive*, but that didn't mean she oozed confidence. She still had her doubts and her insecurities, and being in just a swimsuit would make her feel terribly exposed. Vulnerable. And that feeling was something she tried to avoid.

'Would you mind turning around?'

'Of course not.' He turned his back on her so that she could slip off the robe, and for a brief moment she just stood there and gazed at the broad expanse of his bronzed back. At the width of his shoulders and down to his narrow waist, to the swimming trunks that showed a wonderfully toned backside, and then the long, muscly thighs, darkened by fine hair.

Would he chance a look at her?

No. He's not like that.

Krystiana quickly tugged off the robe and slipped into the pool.

He turned when he heard her moving in the water and slipped in next to her. 'All right?'

She nodded. The water had felt cold at first, but now she was in she realised it was perfect.

'How do you feel about putting your face in the water?'

She looked at its rippling surface. 'I won't be able to see anything.'

He nodded, understanding her fear. 'I have goggles.' He reached over to the steps behind him, where a pair hung. 'Best to wet your hair first, before you put them on.'

She nodded, dipping her head back until the full length of her braid was dripping.

'Here.'

He stepped towards her and she had to suck in a breath as he stood close, helping her with the goggles. They were a bit loose, so he tightened them for her. She was just inches away from his marvellous masculine form and she didn't know where to look. Or to put her hands. He was wearing almost nothing.

'I must look silly.' She blushed.

'You look perfect. So, do you want to try putting your face underwater now? Take a breath and then just lower yourself down for a moment and see what it's like.'

'Okay.' She sucked in a couple of deep breaths before pinching her nose and lowering herself beneath the water's surface.

The world sounded strange from underneath. Muffled and weird. She could see Matteo's ripped abs and long legs, his feet standing sure on the bottom of the pool. She took a quick glance at his shorts, at the line of hair from his belly button that disappeared beneath the fabric.

She stood up again with a rush.

'How was that?'

'Fine.' She lifted the goggles onto her forehead and laughed, blushing. 'It was good!'

He smiled back, clearly enjoying her success. *'Fantastic.* I'll get you a float.'

She watched as he easily heaved his form from the pool, the water rushing down his body, and fetched her a blue square of solid foam from the side before he hopped back in.

'Right—now you're going to try to glide.'

'Glide?'

'You're going to hold this float in front of you. Arms nice and straight, face in the water. And with your feet you're going to push off from the wall and see how far you can glide across the pool.'

That sounded simple enough. 'Okay...'

'Deep breath, face down, then push.'

'Sounds like you want me to give birth.'

He smiled, clearly following her line of thought. To give birth you had to be pregnant, and to be pregnant you had to have had *sex*.

She felt tingles inside. Her belly was fluttering and she was beginning to realise that she was *enjoying* this. Something she'd been dreading since he'd suggested it.

Sucking in a breath, she held the float in front of her, put her face down and pushed off the wall behind her. She surged forward, gliding swiftly and surely through the water until her breath ran out, and then she stood up suddenly, gasping for air. 'I did it!'

'You did! You're a natural! Do it again. But this time kick with your feet as you're gliding.'

'Okay.'

She made her way back to the side of the pool and carried out his instructions, and this time she made it almost halfway across.

'I'm doing it! Did you see?'

'I did! Try it again.'

She did it over and over again, kicking her way all the way across the pool, occasionally lifting her head for a gasp of air, until she reached the other side.

'Teach me something else!'

'Okay. Let's try it without the float.'

'Without?' She wasn't too sure about that. How would she stay on top of the water?

'Yes. Watch me.'

She watched him dip under the water and push off from the wall, and smiled in relief as his body naturally drifted up and glided across the surface, before he stood once again to look at her.

He brushed his wet hair back from his face. 'Easy—see?'

'Easy for *you*, maybe.'

'Have faith, Krystiana. See if you can swim out this far to me.'

He was just over the halfway mark. Technically, it wasn't that far, and she knew that with the goggles she'd be able to see under water just how far away he was. He could be with her in a second if it went wrong.

'I'm trusting you to catch me if I start to drown.'

'You won't drown. You can do this.'

'Okay.'

She adjusted her goggles once again, then sucked in a deep breath and tried to do what she'd seen Matteo do. Head under, push off the wall, kick with her feet, hands out in front of her... Under the water, she could see him. His reassuring torso, his hands out in front of him, ready to reach for her when she got close.

And she made it!

Grabbing his hands and feeling him pull her towards him, she got to her feet, laughing and beaming with joy. 'I did it! Did you see me?'

'You were great!'

He was holding her close. Her hands lay wet and warm upon his chest. And suddenly she realised she was staring into his eyes, and he into hers. Their bodies were touching and she gazed up at his lips, studded with water droplets, and realised, intensely, that she wanted to kiss them so very much.

The realisation hit her with the force of a wave and she glanced up at his eyes to gauge what he was thinking. She thought she saw the same desire in his gaze, too.

The desire, *the need*, to kiss him was just so strong, and as they closed the gap between them, inching ever closer, infinitesimally, she felt her heart pound and the blood roar around her body as if in triumph.

He'll hurt you. Everybody hurts you.

She silenced the voice. Not wanting to hear it. Not in this moment. Not right now. All she wanted right now was…

His lips touched hers and she sank against him, feeling her body come alive. Every nerve-ending was sending sparks. Her heart was pounding with exhilaration at the feel of him beneath her hands as she pulled her even closer.

Nothing else mattered there and then. To be swept away like this was indescribable. The real world dissolved. Fears were silenced. And the hot, sultry desire that she'd tamped down for so long was given free rein.

'Krystiana?'

Matteo's voice called to her as she hurried to her quarters, her hair still dripping.

She turned. 'Yes?'

Stop blushing. Why am I blushing? Oh, yes, I just kissed a prince!

'I forgot to say, what with…' His cheeks reddened and he looked uncomfortable. 'My father has invited you to the ball tonight.'

Her heart sank. 'Ball?'

'It happens every year.'

'Oh.'

She didn't have any outfit suitable for a ball. But how to get out of it without upsetting anyone? Events were moving far too swiftly for her right now. That kiss in the pool had been madness!

'I...er...don't have anything suitable to wear for a ball.'

'I'll get some dresses sent to your rooms for you to try.'

'Erm...'

'Or Mara might have something you could borrow?'

She nodded. 'Okay.'

'Excellent. I'll see you later, then?'

She watched him walk away, wondering just what the hell she was doing...

CHAPTER NINE

MATTEO SAT SWIRLING the wine around in his glass, mesmerised by its movement and colour, though not yet having touched a drop. He just needed to do something with his hands—anything, really—to keep his mind off that moment in the pool with Krystiana.

I kissed her.

She'd emerged from the water, smiling, laughing, so pleased with her progress, and she'd lifted her goggles onto her forehead and beamed at him—a smile that had gone straight to his heart and made it beat like a jackhammer against his ribs. And something—something he hadn't been able to fight—had taken over his common sense and all reason and logic and he'd somehow convinced himself that just one kiss would be okay!

Hah!

He'd fought against it. They'd only known each other for such a short time, and he'd been determined since returning from his kidnapping not to get involved with anyone. Was he so weak? That all it took was a nice smile and a long braid and a shared experience to make his resolve crumble?

He thought over their time together, looking for clues. When had he first begun to succumb to her charms? But he couldn't see the exact moment. He couldn't discern it at all and that frustrated him.

Krystiana had looked at him in shock afterwards. Had quickly waded away from him, clambered up the pool steps, apologising all the way.

No matter what had happened, he'd not wanted things to be awkward between them. He'd wanted to put it right. So he'd chased after her and *asked her to the ball*—as if his mouth had been operating on a different system to his brain.

It hadn't been his place to invite her, and he hadn't meant to ask, but he hadn't been able to bear her running from him like that. He'd wanted to apologise, to put things right, but when she'd turned to face him the invitation had popped out instead.

Matteo pulled the cord that would summon Sergio, and when his servant arrived he asked him to fetch him a canvas and paints. Sergio bowed and disappeared, returning about thirty minutes later with the equipment he needed. Painting the garden had felt good before. Freeing. It had eased his mind and he needed that right now.

He set up the easel out on the sun terrace and thought about how he felt inside. And then, using his fingers, as he had before, he began to daub the surface of the canvas with paint.

He was so carried away with what he was doing he almost didn't hear the footsteps behind him, and he started somewhat when Sergio spoke.

'Dr Szenac, Your Majesty.'

Matteo turned, shocked to see her standing there, but he smiled, glad to see her. Glad that she didn't seem to have been made uncomfortable by what had happened.

'You caught me. I thought I'd try this thing again.'

She smiled back, but it was brief. Fleeting.

'That's good. That you're getting something from it. Those colours look great, but you were great with them last time, so…'

He could sense she had something to say. 'Are you all right?'

'I'm going to leave.'

His heart thudded painfully and the smile dropped from his face. 'What? Why? Because of what happened in the pool? I'm sorry if I've made you uncomfortable, I—'

'I'm going to a hotel. I need to take back control of my life, Matteo. It's slipping away from me here.'

He didn't know what to say. Had he caused this? By kissing her? She had to know that it had been an accident. That it wouldn't happen again.

But those words weren't said. He couldn't. It wasn't as if he was going to beg her to stay. Princes didn't beg. He had to respect her decision, and it was probably best in the long run anyway. Neither of them needed to get involved.

He felt the need to preserve his dignity and he lifted his chin. 'When will you go?'

'Tomorrow morning. I just thought it polite to let you know. As you were so kind as to let me into your home.'

'It was the right thing…' There was more he wanted to say but he was struck dumb, the words caught in his throat. He couldn't say any of them out loud. The one person who soothed his soul, who made him feel he could genuinely smile again, was going because he'd screwed up?

'It's for the best. For both of us, I think,' she said.

He agreed. It was for the best. But he didn't feel ready. He'd thought he'd still got weeks left with her. Weeks in which they would talk and develop their friendship. In which to get her out of his system. But for her to leave now, so abruptly… Because he'd overstepped a line he'd never intended to cross…

This was why he didn't get involved with people any more. Relationships got complicated.

'I'll always consider you my friend, Krystiana. I hope our…moment hasn't jeopardised that.'

She shook her head. 'It hasn't. I've always felt connected to you and I think I always will. It's been an honour to know you.'

He nodded.

She seemed to want to say something more, but no more words were forthcoming. Was she struggling to speak as much as he? Did she want him to fight for her to stay? Or just to let her go? *What do I want?*

She nodded a goodbye and walked away.

Matteo swore to himself, his anger and frustration rising. He turned back to his painting, looked at the happy colours, the swirls of green and yellow. His palette lay off to one side and he dipped his hand in black and swept his hand across the canvas. The black cut a swathe through the light—sorrow darkening the joy.

And he stared at it until his anger abated.

'Which one do you want to try first?' Mara spread her hand out at the array of dresses she'd hung up on the rail she had prepped for Krystiana. 'I think the blue would really bring out your eyes.'

Krystiana was in no mood for any colour bringing out anything. Least of all her eyes. She didn't want anyone to notice her. Didn't want anyone to see the sadness that was in her soul.

'What about the black one?'

Mara looked at her as if she was crazy. 'The black one? No, no, *no*, Krystiana! The black is too safe. It's wrong for you. How about the red?'

No. Red would be too much. Everybody would look at her.

'What about that one?'

Mara hefted it from the rail. 'This one? I think this one will look lovely on you. Try it on!'

Krystiana took it, draping the pale grey silk over her arm and going into the bedroom to try it.

The grey was perfect. Almost silver, but not quite. Sleeveless and with a sweetheart neckline. It was understated. The kind of dress that wouldn't make her stand out. And despite it having been designed for Mara, who was sylph-like in build, it fitted Krystiana perfectly, moulding her curves.

She twisted and turned in front of the mirror, admiring it but telling herself to not get too excited. Tonight, she would hug the wall, a glass of wine in her hand, which she probably wouldn't drink, and after an hour or so she would slip away, unnoticed.

She was sad that she had made the decision to leave, but it was for the best. Matteo was getting too close. Getting under her skin. And she didn't know what to do with that!

She'd kissed him in the pool.

She could feel her attraction for him growing and it hurt. Pained her that she could do nothing about it because it wouldn't be right. Getting involved with a man like him... Losing control... Giving him power over her...

If she went into a relationship with a powerful man like him she'd lose. Her heart and her soul. She'd be open and out of control. That short kiss had shown her how out of control she had become in such a small amount of time. One kiss and already she'd knocked down the walls keeping him out.

He belonged to his people, not her, and if she tried to be with him in any way the media would want to know who she was. They would begin to dig into her background and her life—her history would be revealed to all.

No one on Isla Tamoura except for Aunt Carolina and Matteo knew about her past, and that was how she wanted it to stay. She had built a new life here. People didn't look at her with the knowledge of her past in their eyes. She wasn't pitied. She wasn't asked about it and that was the way she wanted it.

'How does it look?' Mara called from the other room. 'I hope you're going to show me.'

Krystiana pulled open the door and stepped out, smiling at Mara's obvious glee. 'What do you think? Does it look all right?'

Mara gazed at her in awe. *'È bellissimo!'*

'It's not too much?'

'No! You look breathtaking.'

Krystiana gazed down at the gown and bit her lip, reconsidering. She didn't want to look 'breathtaking'. At all.

'No, no! Don't look like that. You're wearing it. I've even got a clutch to match it. And shoes. What size are you?'

Krystiana told her.

'Perfect! You'll be the belle of the ball!'

'I don't want to be the belle. I'm not a guest of honour—just a friend, that's all.'

'Oh, come, now. That's *not* all!'

She frowned. 'What do you mean?'

'You like him, yes?'

Krystiana blushed madly. She couldn't tell Mara! Mara had once been his *wife*!

'Not like that.'

Mara raised an eyebrow. 'I wish I could believe you.'

'There's nothing between us. In fact, I'm leaving tomorrow.'

'You're leaving?' Mara looked shocked.

'Tomorrow morning. I have to.'

Mara nodded. 'Maybe that's wise…'

Krystiana turned away and began to unzip the dress. Even Mara could see that she and Matteo would be a bad thing.

Mara laid a hand upon her arm, stilling her. 'I know it will hurt you to leave.'

'It's the best thing for both of us.'

Mara nodded her head solemnly. 'It's a pity, but I admire you for being so sensible.'

'I'm not being sensible. I don't know *what* I'm being.'

'What do you feel for him?'

Krystiana blinked. Unsure how to answer. 'I like him. Maybe too much,' she said.

Mara nodded. 'He's easy to like. Easy to love.'

Krystiana stared at her. 'I don't *love* him, Mara.'

That was just ridiculous!

She'd read somewhere that when you felt attracted to someone you could blame your medial prefrontal cortex, because that was the part of the brain that was responsible for any *love at first sight* activity. The inferior temporal cortex reacted to visual stimuli, the orbitofrontal cortex reacted emotionally, the anterior cingulate cortex caused physiological responses and the right insula dictated arousal.

Basically, it meant that most of your brain was going overboard, so no wonder you couldn't think straight!

But as she got ready in her room, trying to sort out her hair and make-up for this, her last evening at the palace, she tried to tell herself that she was doing the right thing—even though she strongly suspected her thoughts and decisions were based on her emotional responses.

She liked Matteo. More than she should. So getting away from him was the obvious solution. Besides, he probably wouldn't want to speak to her much tonight, anyway. She'd clearly shocked him when she'd told him she was leaving, so perhaps tonight would be okay? They could avoid each other all evening.

She put in her diamond drop earrings and stood in front of the mirror, checking her reflection. The grey dress was actually very beautiful. Understated and classic. It was a pity it was on loan, because she loved it very much.

Krystiana checked her watch. Nearly time to go.

Why do I feel so nervous?

There was a tentative knock at her door and,

suspecting it was Sergio, she went and opened it. Only it wasn't Sergio at all.

It was Matteo.

Her heart leapt into her throat when she saw him standing there in dinner jacket and black bow tie. He looked gorgeous! She almost took a step back. Not sure why he was here.

'I've come to escort you to the ball. On your last night here with you as our guest it seemed right. No hard feelings?'

'Oh. Right. Okay.'

'We're okay?'

She nodded. 'Absolutely. I can't thank you enough for all that you've done for me.'

Matteo gave her a short smile. 'You look *bellissimo*. Truly.'

She flushed at the compliment. 'Thank you. So do you.'

He held out his arm for her to slip her hand through, and they walked arm in arm down the palace corridors.

For a few moments she felt quite awkward, being with him. She'd not expected him to come to her door, but he was most certainly a gentleman and clearly he didn't want an unescorted lady arriving at the ball. He was wearing some kind of scent that was playing havoc with her olfactory senses, so she tried a bit of mouth-breathing to try and calm them down.

'How many people are going to be there?'

'A few hundred.'

A few *hundred*…

'Where is the ball being held?'

'In the White Room.'

'I don't think I've been there.'

'We use it only for the most special of occasions.'

She nodded, walking alongside him, trying not to think that this might be the last time they'd be together. Trying not to think of how much she liked him. How much he might think that she was running away. Because she didn't like to think that she was.

'Will Mara and Alex be there? So I can say goodbye?'

'Of course.'

'Great. That's…great.' She didn't *feel* great. She felt sad. But she had to do the right thing.

A few hundred.

He stopped suddenly. 'I think I should leave you here. If we arrived together it would send out the wrong message.'

'Maybe you're right.'

She was wrong for him. He was trying to tell her that. The kiss in the pool had been a blip on both their parts. They couldn't be anything more. It had just been physical.

She nodded. 'I'd rather everyone assumed I was just a normal guest. Nothing to do with you.'

Which I'm not.

He removed his arm from hers and straightened his jacket. 'And of course I'd hate to throw you to the wolves. The press,' he explained.

'Exactly. I'd rather stay out of the papers.' Though that was the least of her worries. She'd rather stay as far away from him as she could because she just didn't trust her physical reactions to him.

He smiled ruefully. 'You promise not to leave without saying goodbye?'

'I promise,' she said, hating every word, knowing that deep in her heart she longed to be in his arms and held by him, pressed close, cherished and adored. Their kiss in the pool might have been the biggest mistake she'd ever made, but it had felt so good! And that was why it was so confusing.

'I don't want you to leave without a chance to…'

She got sucked into the hypnotic gaze of his eyes. 'Chance to what?'

She saw the hesitation in his eyes. The fight within him. And then he was stepping close.

He reached up to stroke the side of her face. 'I feel like I know who you are. And that I'll never meet anyone else like you again. I'm not sure I want to lose you.'

Krystiana sucked in a breath, trying to steady her racing heart. 'I…'

'You feel it, too.'

'Matteo…'

And suddenly his mouth was on hers.

She closed her eyes in ecstasy. Giving herself one more moment of bliss. A single moment in which she'd allow herself to take what he could give.

Her hands lay upon his chest and she could feel his heart pounding, the muscles beneath his skin, the way he wrapped himself around her as he pulled her closer still.

Her logical mind was screaming at her to stop, but she couldn't. She silenced the voice. No, that was wrong. The voice disappeared. Because all she wanted to experience was the feeling of his lips upon hers. Her body pressed against his. The fire building in her soul. The heat that was searing her skin, making every nerve-ending electric.

She'd never felt this before. Never been like this with anyone before. Not like this. There'd been awkward fumbles and kisses from guys she'd not felt such attraction for, and with Adamo it had been good, but with Matteo it was a fierce thing—a force that powered through her like a hurricane. Unstoppable and unrelenting.

As the kiss deepened and her tongue entwined with his she groaned in delight, cradling his face in her hands, feeling the soft bristles of his beard beneath her skin. She knew she wanted more. Oh, so much more… But…

They broke apart and stared at each other, both surprised, both overwhelmed by what had just happened. Stunned.

Her fear at what would happen when she had to leave had just been made worse! Kissing him had just made it a lot harder.

Why am I doing this to myself? What on earth is going on?

Krystiana looked up and down the palace corridors but no one was around. This was just between her and Matteo.

'I'm sorry. We…er…shouldn't have done that.'

'No.'

'But we keep doing it.'

'Yes.'

'Why? Why would we punish ourselves like this?' She was almost in tears. Could hear it in her voice.

He took a step back. 'I'm sorry. I don't mean to. It's just that when I'm with you…'

'What?' She needed to know what was driving him. What was causing him to keep kissing her. Because then it might make sense to her why she kept kissing *him*.

He frowned and took a step towards her, his gaze dropping to her mouth before he looked back up at her eyes.

'I'll see you in the ballroom.'

The White Room was exactly that. White walls and ceiling. A white marble floor. Columns thick as tree trunks like silver birches, pulling the gaze upwards towards numerous crystal chandeliers. Huge gold vases held swathes of white lilies, roses and jasmine.

As she descended the steps towards the milling crowds, accepting a flute of champagne from a server, Krystiana hoped she could lose herself in the crowd. Even if she *did* feel there was a huge neon arrow above her head, lit up with the message *I just kissed your prince!*

She felt torn. And exhilarated. Confused and trapped. Could the whole world see the imprint of his lips on hers? Was it written all over her face? Heat and lust and secrets?

I should have known better!

She was muddled in her thinking. Being with Matteo stopped her brain from working properly. She really felt something for him, and it wasn't just attraction—it was something more than that. Krystiana had never wanted to be with a guy as much as she wanted to be with him. She had never felt more attracted to someone in her life.

This was new territory for her! Uncharted, dangerous territory, with someone who was forbidden!

Or was he?

Now that she'd kissed him, now that she'd tasted a little of what he had to offer, a new voice was suggesting that maybe she should enjoy it. Maybe it was all right. Maybe, just maybe, he *was* the man for her...

Perhaps that was why it was so confusing—because she was fighting something that she should just accept. But how would she know for sure? How would she know she was safe giving him her heart? It had never worked before when she had done that. She couldn't think of one relationship in her life that worked well. Well, except for with Dr Bonetti. They loved one another. But they were from the same world.

Krystiana took a sip of her champagne, intending only to take a small swallow, but downing the whole thing in one. Surprised, she passed her empty glass to another server and took another full glass, determined to go slower with this one.

If two people were attracted to one another then why shouldn't they make something of it? Why shouldn't they act on their attraction? They were grown adults. They could make their own decisions.

He'd been through the same things as her. The

same scares, the same terrors, the same fears. He knew how she felt and she him. Where would she find *that* again?

Sighing, she sipped her champagne, stopping only to turn at the fanfare of trumpets as an official announced the entry of His Majesty King Alberto and his son, Crown Prince Matteo.

She stared up at him from her place in the crowd and could see the certainty and assuredness on Matteo's face, trapped within a practised smile. She saw the way his gaze coasted all around him, oozing authority and power as he descended the steps into the room, and how he stayed a few steps behind his father, honouring royal etiquette.

She glanced at Alberto. The King she'd met just once. A tall, proud man, he was greeting a long line of people, smiling and shaking hands. He looked a little more drawn than before. A bit grey... He carried a heavy weight upon his shoulders—perhaps it was that?

He was soon to abdicate. And happily, by all accounts. Krystiana had no doubt that Matteo would make a fabulous king. He was strong and steady. Overflowing with charitable, selfless acts that his people adored him for.

As do I.

Matteo would make an excellent leader for his

country. All that he had been through had only
served to make him stronger.

The King got to the end of his long line of
meet-and-greet people and stepped up to a white
podium which was adorned with the Romano
royal coat of arms—a gold shield, with a sword
at its centre, flanked by a lion on one side and a
unicorn on the other, both rearing up as if honouring the sword.

The room went quiet.

The King looked about him, waiting for his
moment. The ultimate public speaker. 'Ladies
and gentlemen of the court, nothing makes me
happier than to see you all here—though my
happiness is tinged with a little sadness that this
will be the final ball I will host as King. But my
successor is one you all know, love and respect,
and I know that he will follow the honour, tradition and heritage of this fine land. My only
son—Matteo.'

The crowd clapped, smiling broadly.

'We all know his story. For those of us left
behind it was an unsettling time. We were cast
adrift, uncertain, unknowing. We tried what we
could to ensure his safe return, but each time—
as you know—the guerrillas who held him
proved not to be reputable people and they kept
him from us. Matteo did not get to see the birth
of his daughter. He did not get to see her early

years or experience the joy that we did as she began to sit up, then crawl, then walk. Nor did he hear her first word, but I'm sure he was very pleased to hear it was "Papà".'

He smiled at his son, who stood proudly by his side.

'But we did get him back, and he has proved his strength and fortitude. Returning strong and unhurt by his time away, for which we are very grateful. Tonight I would like to name this ball in his honour, and also to announce some incredible news.'

The crowd inched forward, eager to hear it.

Behind the King, Krystiana saw Matteo's smile falter somewhat as he turned his gaze to his father. Clearly Matteo did not know what the King was about to say.

'It has been decided that in anticipation of Matteo taking the throne next year, he will go on a six-week tour of the kingdom of Tamoura, visiting every major city and every urban centre, meeting the people and showing the world that no one can beat down the strength and courage that my son has. He will be a *strong* king! A king committed to the welfare of his people. Hopefully, he will meet as many of them as he can. His full itinerary will be posted tomorrow at the royal court and the tour will begin in one week's time!'

Matteo's smile broadened, as if he'd already known this would be the King's proclamation, but she knew better. She could see the surprise in his eyes.

He didn't know about this.

She was shocked, too. He was leaving the palace. Perhaps it was a good thing that she was packing up tomorrow, because if she'd stayed her heart would have been broken anyway. He would be leaving on a tour of the isle. No doubt with a jam-packed itinerary. He would be returning to the world where he lived and she... She would be returning to hers. She had patients. He had subjects.

The bubble was popping. She'd always known that it would. She would have popped it herself tomorrow. This would push him. Prepare him for kingship. It would be a good thing for him. Good for her, too. Because if he was leaving in just one week, then she could leave knowing that his mind would not be on her departure, but on his travelling arrangements.

You see? We never would have had a chance. I was right to stop this.

She tried to make herself feel happy about that, but she was struggling.

The King stepped back to hold out a hand to his son and Matteo stepped forward to take it. As he clasped his son's hand and pulled him into a hug the crowd began to cheer and applaud.

But their cries of joy quickly changed to cries of shock as King Alberto slumped in his son's arms, his face pale and sweaty, and Matteo had to lower him gently to the ground…

'Call for an ambulance!'

Matteo couldn't believe that this was happening. What was wrong with his father?

Holding his father fast, he stared at his slack face. 'Papà, hang on—don't you die on me!'

Behind him, he heard a commotion as someone pushed their way through the crowd and he heard her voice.

'Excuse me! Excuse me—please, make way…'

And then there she was. Krystiana. Kneeling down on the floor beside his father, a pool of grey silk around her as she assessed the situation, her fingers at his neck, assessing for a pulse.

'Okay, he's breathing—that's good.' She quickly unbuttoned the King's jacket and laid her ear against his chest and listened. 'Does someone have a watch? With a second hand?'

A man Matteo didn't know offered one and he passed it to Krystiana, who kept her gaze on it as she listened to the King's chest once again.

'He has tachycardia.'

Matteo frowned. 'What?'

'A fast heartbeat. Too fast. We need to get him to hospital, where they can give him some drugs or a shock to bring it back down.'

Servants arrived in droves to usher the guests into another room so that the paramedics could come in, get the King on a trolley and attach electrodes to his chest to monitor his heartbeat. It was one hundred and fifty-two beats per minute.

'Papà, you're going to be all right.'

The King took his son's hand in his. 'I'm okay…'

The paramedics looked to Matteo. 'Are you coming in the ambulance?'

He nodded. 'Yes. So is she.' He pointed at Krystiana, who looked shocked to be included.

'Then, let's go!'

Matteo and Krystiana followed the paramedics down the long palatial corridors and out to the ambulance. Thankfully their arrival had been through the rear gates, so hopefully there wouldn't be too much about this in the press the next day. Besides, it was just a fast heartbeat. He wasn't having a heart attack or anything. They'd get him sorted out at the hospital.

As they got on board Krystiana looked at the ECG tracing. 'It looks like he has atrial fibrillation.'

'What does that mean?' Matteo asked, needing to know everything that was going on.

'It's the upper chambers of the heart. The atria. They're creating irregular impulses that are rapid and uncoordinated.'

'What does that mean for my father?'

She shrugged. 'It could be a temporary thing and stop on its own, but he might need assistance to stop it.'

'How?'

'Drugs. A shock to the heart.'

'An electric shock? But why now? What's caused it?'

'I don't know, Matteo. I don't know your father's health history. Does he have high blood pressure?'

'I don't think so. He hasn't mentioned anything.'

'Heart disease?'

'No. Papà, how do you feel?'

'Like something is trying to jump out of my chest.'

'Are you in pain?'

'No, it just feels...*weird*.'

'We're nearly there. Hang on.'

He felt Krystiana lay a reassuring hand upon his shoulder.

The paramedics kept on observing the trace, monitoring his father's blood pressure and pulse rate, and Krystiana had placed an oxygen mask over the King's face, murmuring to him to try and control his breathing, to remain as calm as he could. Before he knew what was happening they were pulling up at the private entrance the royals used at the hospital.

They wheeled his father in and got him hooked up to another heart machine as the paramedics relayed what had happened to the attending physician.

The doctor told the King that they would give him a beta-blocker to try and get his heart-rate below ninety beats per minute.

'You might feel some tiredness, and your hands and feet may get cold. We'll monitor your blood pressure continuously and see how you get on.'

'*Grazie.*'

'You must just rest for a while.'

'*Si.*'

Matteo had expected more action. This was his father's *heart*! Could he die?

'Why aren't you doing more?' he asked the doctor.

'We're doing what we can. We have to see if the medication will bring down the heart-rate.'

'And if it doesn't? How long do we leave it?'

'Matteo, give them time,' Krystiana said, her voice soothing and calm.

He glanced at her, saw the concern on her face and knew instinctively that she was right. They didn't need him interfering and asking too many questions or getting in the way. This was their territory. They were the ones who knew best.

'Matteo...?' His father held out his hand to him.

'*Si*, Papà?'

'I think I might have to hand over to you earlier than suspected.' He smiled, his eyes sad.

What? No! That wasn't what Matteo wanted to hear. Become King? *No.* His father still had years left in him. Didn't he?

'No, you won't. This is just a blip, Papà. You'll be back home tomorrow—just you wait and see.'

'No, I fear not. There may be some things I have kept from you...'

Matteo frowned.

'Dr Szenac? Would you mind if I spoke to my son alone?' his father asked.

Krystiana nodded and stood up. 'Of course. Take all the time you need.' And she stepped out of the private room, closing the door quietly behind her.

Matteo turned back to his father, apprehension and fear filling his heart. 'What is it?'

'I wasn't sure when would be the best time to tell you...but...when you were away I got ill. The cardio doctors believed it was stress brought on by your kidnapping.'

Cardio. The heart. An ice-cold lump settled in his stomach.

'What happened?'

'I had a heart attack.'

He stood up in shock. *'What?'*

'It was minor, Matteo, but I needed bypass surgery. You see this scar line?'

Matteo frowned as he stared at his father's chest. His father was quite hairy, and he almost couldn't see it. The scar that ran from just below the dip in his throat down to the bottom of the sternum.

'Why didn't you tell me?'

His father shrugged. 'I was always going to abdicate when I turned seventy—you know that. When you were taken I had no idea where you were. My only son. My only child. The stress of everything... The day you were returned to us was the greatest in my entire life! For a moment, I thought Alexandra would have to take the throne!'

He tried to laugh. But it fell flat in the small room.

Matteo stared at the scar. A mark that showed his father to be frailer than he'd realised. Not the invincible, strong man he'd believed him to be but human, just like the rest of them.

'You should have told me. How did you manage to keep this from me?'

'I swore everyone to secrecy. Why upset you? You had just come home, learned that your mother was dead and your marriage was over! I couldn't tell you about this, too! I was protecting you, believing I would last until your coronation anyway. Honestly, I thought you would never have to find out. And I'm sorry that you have.'

Above his father's head, the machine beeped out the fast heartbeat. The drugs didn't seem to be working. Matteo felt doubt and fear. He couldn't lose his father.

'*Ti amo*, Papà.'

'I love you, too. Now, let me rest awhile.'

'All right. I'll just be outside—but buzz if you need *anything*. Okay?'

'I will. Go now.'

He kissed his father on the cheek and left the room. As soon as he saw Krystiana all the emotion he had been feeling came to the fore and he felt tears burning his eyes. He went straight into her outstretched arms.

Being held by her, being close to her, made him feel comforted. She was warm and loving and he knew that she cared for him. She *had* to. Ever since that kiss they'd shared… It hadn't been one-sided. She'd responded too. And now she was the one to comfort him, to make him feel safe. He'd always felt safe with her, and *safe* was a good thing after two years of never knowing if you'd get to see tomorrow's sunrise.

She sat him down. 'Are you all right?'

He told her everything his father had said about his prior heart condition. The heart attack. The bypass.

She sat listening, nodding occasionally. 'That makes sense. Fibrillation like that can often be caused if there's a prior heart condition.'

'Will he be all right, do you think?'

'It's a long time since I worked on a cardiac ward, Matteo. I'd hate to say the wrong thing. But what we *do* know is that he's in the safest place he can be. Where his heart-rate will be continually monitored.'

'When should the drugs take effect? The rate was still high.'

'They should have worked by now, really. He might need shocking. They might give him amiodarone... I'm not sure.'

He took her hand in his. 'I'm glad you're here.'

She smiled back uncertainly. 'I'll stay for as long as you need me.'

He was glad to hear it. His foundations had been rocked and he needed an anchor. He didn't know what it was that was flooding through him, these feelings for her—feelings that he'd never expected to have again. But the thought of losing her whilst his father teetered on the edge of an abyss… *No*. It would be too much.

He reached forward to stroke the side of her face. 'Thank you. There's something about you, Krystiana… I don't know what it is, but…'

She was looking deeply into his eyes, their souls connecting. 'Don't say any more.'

He nodded. 'Thank you.'

He narrowed the distance between them and felt his lips connect with hers. He'd craved her ever since he'd last kissed her, but that kiss had been different. This one was gentle and slow, savouring every moment, every movement. She tasted of champagne, and her honeyed scent stimulated his senses into overdrive. He wanted so much more…

He barely knew what was happening in his world right now. But he was looking for comfort.

Matteo's father was sitting upright in his bed, looking nervous. The doctors had placed pads on his chest and were going to try and shock his rhythm back to normality.

'Will it hurt?'

'Yes, but not for long. And if it works you'll feel much better almost instantly.'

'Good. All right. Go ahead.'

He laid his head back and the doctor pressed

a button that lowered the pillow end of the bed. He had to be flat for this.

Once he was lying flat, the doctor looked about him. 'Charging…stand clear…*shocking.*'

King Alberto's body flinched violently and then he groaned, relaxing back onto the sheets.

Krystiana looked at the heart monitor, but his heart-rate remained high. She felt for the King. This couldn't be good at all.

'Charging. Stand clear. *Shocking.*'

Again the King's body went into violent spasm and then collapsed again, but this time the heart-rate began to drop and finally went down to eighty-four beats per minute.

The cardio doctor smiled at Matteo. 'We have sinus rhythm.'

Matteo reached for his father's hand. 'It's done, Papà, you're going to be okay.'

Alberto smiled wearily at his son. *'Grazie a Dio!'*

'We'll keep monitoring your father overnight, but if he maintains his rhythm I see no reason why he can't be up and about tomorrow.'

The cardio doctor shook Matteo's hand, smiled at Krystiana and then left the room.

Krystiana sat down in the chair opposite Matteo and smiled, happy for him and his father. She knew how much he needed his dad. Knew that connection. She missed her own—or she

missed the father she'd *believed* she'd had before
he took her. That father—pre-kidnapping—had
been someone she'd idolised.

Afterwards…after all she'd been through…
their relationship had been spoiled. She'd had no
father to come home to. And every time she'd
turned on the television she'd seen her father's
face. Every time she'd opened a newspaper there
had seemed to be a new story about him and his
'unstable mind-set', according to ex-girlfriends
and old enemies who had all earned a few *zloty*
selling their stories.

When she'd gone back to school everyone
had treated her differently. Even the teachers.
All she'd wanted was normality. To be treated
as she had always been treated. But all the kids
had suddenly wanted to be her friend. To be invited back to her house so they could examine
the home that had once belonged to Piotr Szenac.

Even her own mother had begun acting
strangely, and she'd felt a distance between them.
A distance that had puzzled her—because surely
her mother had wanted her back? She'd fought
for custody of Krystiana.

And then she'd died. Less than a year after
Krystiana had come home Nikola Szenac had
been hit by a bus. Krystiana had been fetched
from her school lessons to be told by the head-
mistress. And then she'd been alone in the world,

struggling to understand all that had happened, until Aunt Carolina had reached out to save her.

And now here she sat, an orphaned girl from Poland, beside the bed of the King of Isla Tamoura.

'We should get something to eat. It's late.' Matteo stood up and kissed his father's cheek. 'Is there anything you want me to bring tomorrow?'

Alberto smiled. 'Some decent pyjamas would be good. These hospital gowns are a bit itchy.'

'Nonsense! I'm sure they are the finest cotton.'

'Hmm… You're not wearing one, though, are you?'

'Fair point. Goodnight, Papà. Krystiana and I will be back in the morning.'

Alberto turned to look at her curiously. 'I must thank you, Dr Szenac, for saving my life.'

She shook her head. 'I didn't do anything. Not really.'

'You looked after me *and* my son. I am grateful you were with us.'

She smiled. He was a good old man. A good father. 'I'm glad you're feeling better, Your Majesty.'

'Call me Alberto.'

She blushed. That didn't seem right. He was the King of Isla Tamoura! Calling him by his first name was intimate. For friends and family. She wasn't family—so did he consider her a friend?

'Thank you, Your Majesty.'

He smiled. 'Go and get some sleep. It's been a long day.'

'It has. Yes. You too—sleep well.'

'I'm sure I will. Now you go and do the same.'

CHAPTER TEN

ONCE THEY WERE back in the palace Matteo couldn't help but pull her close, savouring the feel of her in his arms. He'd nearly lost his father. But she was still here and he needed her closeness and comfort.

'You were my rock tonight. I don't know how I would have got through it without you.'

'You'd have survived. You'd have had no choice.'

'I guess not.' He looked at her and stroked her hair. It was so soft.

'You need to get some sleep,' she said.

'Are you prescribing that?'

She smiled. 'I am.'

'Perhaps you could help me sleep tonight?' he asked, with intent.

She knew exactly what he meant. But was he suggesting it for the right reasons?

Laughing, she pushed him away, pretending that she had misunderstood. 'I could prescribe you a sleeping tablet.'

'You're not my doctor, though.'

She smiled. 'No. I'm not. All right, why don't you have a mug of warm milk? A warm bath?'

He considered both options. 'I've never enjoyed warm milk, and I take a shower first thing in the morning.' He raised an eyebrow. 'There is another way that you could help me sleep...'

Krystiana could only imagine how wonderful that might be, but someone had to be sensible here. 'And what would that be?'

'You could come with me to my quarters and make sure I get into bed on time?'

She tilted her head to one side, considering it. Trying her hardest not to laugh.

Oh, she wanted to. She could feel her body saying *yes*. 'Perhaps.'

'You could lie in my arms and stroke my hair until I fall asleep.'

She smiled. 'I could.'

'There are many things we could do. I keep fighting this...but I want you in my arms so much, you have no idea.'

She had a very clear idea. She could feel his arousal pressed against her.

He kissed her lips. Then her neck, trailing his mouth delicately down the long, smooth stretch of skin, drinking up her little moan of pleasure. 'I hear that orgasm is a wonderful precursor to a good night's sleep...'

He heard her throaty chuckle and raised his head to look into her eyes, a dreamy smile upon his face.

'Prolactin levels *do* make men sleepy. As does oxytocin and vasopressin—all produced by the brain after sex.'

'I love it when you talk dirty to me.'

She laughed, but then her face grew serious. 'You know, wanting sex is a classic response after someone has experienced the shock of feeling their mortality.'

He raised an eyebrow. 'Is that right?'

'Yes. People want to prove they're vital. What better way of cheating death than to do the very thing that creates life?'

He cocked his head to one side. 'Is that a bad response?'

'Not necessarily. But a woman likes to know that her man wants her because he wants *her* and no other reason—not just because he wants to prove how full of life he is.'

He looked her directly in the eye, so that she was not mistaken. 'I want to be with *you*. Because you've been driving me wild for days and I've not been able to do anything about it. Because I've been fighting it. Telling myself it was the wrong thing to do. But right now I'm not sure I believe any of that. What happened tonight proves that life is short. I want your lips, your kisses, your arms around me. I want your body pressed into mine and to hell with everything else! I might have had a shock tonight, but that shock has taught me that life is meant to be lived—and why should we deny ourselves what we want in life more than anything?'

She smiled.

The press of her curves against his body was almost driving him insane! To hell with tradition and law and being careful! He'd done that for so long, and since coming back from the mountains he had kept a tight control on so much of his feelings and emotions. But he couldn't do that with her. She changed him. Made him want. And need.

And right now he needed her in his arms and in his bed.

She kissed him on the lips. 'Then I'm yours.'

What the hell am I doing?

Acting recklessly. Giving in to her temptations. Not thinking.

Despite everything—despite the fact that he could have anyone he wanted—he wanted *her*, and that knowledge was strangely exciting and powerful. It gave her a thrill. Her heart pounded and her blood hummed with an inner energy that she couldn't explain when she was with him.

As she slipped out of the grey dress lent to her

by Mara she looked at herself in the bathroom mirror and wondered briefly who this woman was. She felt as if so much had changed since she had come here.

Krystiana removed her earrings, her necklace, slipped her feet out of her heels and removed the last of her underwear. On the back of the bathroom door was a robe and she pulled it on, checking her reflection.

I'm ready.

Sucking in a deep breath, she opened the bathroom door and leaned against the doorjamb as she gazed at Matteo, who stood waiting for her beside his bed.

'Are we sure about this?'

'Do we have to be?' he asked, before making his way over to her, his hands cupping her face and pulling her lips towards his once more...

'Good morning.'

'Buongiorno!'

She kissed him, inhaling his lovely male scent of soap and sandalwood. 'Any news from the hospital?'

'He had a restful night.'

'That's great!' she said, even though she knew that the quicker King Alberto recovered, the faster everything would change, throwing them

into turmoil once again. But that was for later.
For a time she wasn't ready to think about.

He must have seen the hesitation in her features. 'What's wrong?'

'Nothing. Honestly, I'm happy for your father.'
'But?'

'But nothing.' How could she tell him? It was
incredibly selfish! What did she want? For his
father to be ill a lot longer?

He smiled and pulled her close for a kiss.

It was heaven. Being kissed by him. Being
held by him. In his arms she just felt so...*adored.*
It was an addictive state, and Krystiana knew
all about addictions, having looked after many
addicts in her time. They constantly craved that
high. That feel-good moment when every worry
and concern just melted away because they were
in a state of bliss. She could understand it a little
more, experiencing this. The high she got being
with him.

'Are you going to the hospital this morning?'

'I thought we could go after breakfast?'

'You want me to come with you?'

'I'm taking Alex to see her grandfather. Mara's
staying here, as she has a business meeting, and
I thought Alex might cheer him up.'

She nodded. Alex brightened everyone's lives.
She was such a cutie. And she would grow up to
be a stunner, she had no doubt. If Krystiana was

going to get to know Matteo, perhaps she ought to get to know his daughter better, too?

'All right. But are you sure you need me in the way? It seems like a family moment.'

He took her hand and squeezed it. 'I want you with me. Now, let's eat. Out on the terrace—it's a wonderful morning.'

Sergio—who appeared to be totally unruffled to find her in Matteo's bedchamber this morning—served them dark, strong espresso, sour cherry *crostatas*, custard-filled *ciambellas* and some *strudel di mele*, alongside a selection of fresh fruits and juices.

'I can feel myself putting on the pounds just looking at this.' Krystiana smiled.

Matteo smiled back at her and reached for her hand, bringing the back of it to his sugared lips and kissing it. 'Eat.'

Mara brought Alex to them, greeting Matteo by kissing both his cheeks and doing the same to Krystiana.

'Give your father all the best from me and tell him I'll be in this afternoon.'

'I will.'

Matteo crouched down to look at his daughter, who smiled at him from behind her mother's legs, holding a bedraggled teddy.

'Hey, Alex! Are you ready to come with me and see Nonno?'

Alex nodded. Smiling, Matteo reached out for her hand and then scooped her up into his arms.

'Saluta tua madre.'

Alex gave her mother a smile and Mara bent down for a kiss. 'You be good for your father.'

Alex nodded, hugging her teddy.

Mara smiled too, and then her eyes narrowed with amusement as she looked at the two of them. 'Something's changed…'

Matteo smiled. 'Just pleased to be with my daughter again, in the knowledge that my father will be back pounding the hallways before we know it.'

'Okay…' But Mara seemed to suspect there was something else. She looked at Krystiana and seemed to come to some conclusion. She raised an eyebrow. 'You're *happy.*'

He laughed. 'Is that so wrong?'

Mara smiled 'Being happy? No. Not at all. Remember to say hi to your father for me.'

'I will.'

She kissed her daughter and walked away.

Today was going to be a *good* day. He was going to see his father and then, when he got back, he was going to think about what was happening between him and Krystiana.

It was all moving so fast. And he had done

something he'd told himself not to do. He'd given in to his physical desires and slept with her, and it had been wonderful, mind-blowing, and everything he'd suspected it would be. But where did it leave them? It could never be serious between them. That was against the law—they couldn't marry. And he'd never thought he'd be the type to have a fling, so...

Whatever happened, he wanted to do the right thing. He didn't want to upset Krystiana. He didn't want to confuse Alex about who was in her life and who wasn't. And nor did he want to cause pain to himself.

He strongly suspected he might do that anyway. Either way, whatever it was that they had could not continue for any length of time. The time would come when it would have to end.

The question was, could he end it without hurting her?

Matteo and Alex walked hand in hand into King Alberto's room, Krystiana following dutifully behind.

'Papà! How are you?' Matteo kissed his father on both cheeks.

'Much better, today, Matteo. Now! Do I see a tiny little princess who needs a big hug from her *nonno*?'

He reached out for Alex and the little girl let

go of her father's hand and jumped up into Alberto's grasp.

'Careful, Papà. You're meant to be resting.'

'Holding my granddaughter will do me *good*, Matteo.' Alberto kissed Alex and gave her a little tickle, and her wonderful bright laughter filled the room. 'Oh, and Dr Szenac! You are here, too! Hello! How is my son behaving himself without me there to keep an eye on him?'

Krystiana smiled. 'He's being good.'

'I'm glad to hear it. Though I'm surprised to see you here today. You doctors just can't stay away! You're like vultures!' he said with a laugh.

Krystiana felt her heart pound with nerves as Alberto sat Alex on the bed and passed her a small wrapped gift. 'Here, I got you something. Open it!'

Alex tore through the paper and beamed when she saw a book covered in bright animals. She lay back against her grandfather and began to turn the pages.

'Alex, what do you say to Nonno?'

'Grazie.' Alex smiled shyly at her grandfather.

'Good girl.' Matteo ruffled her hair, smiling at the cute response. 'How on earth did you get her a present?' he asked his father. 'I thought you were on bed rest?'

'One of the perks of being a king, Matteo, and

I needn't tell you, is that I have servants to do my bidding.'

His son smiled. 'Ah… Have the doctors been in to see you yet?'

Alberto nodded. 'Yes. They've checked me out and told me I need to take it easy. Take it *easy*? I run a country, I told them. That's no easy feat.'

Matteo smiled. 'And you do it very well. If I'm half the King that you are then I will consider myself to be lucky.'

'Well, you're going to get the chance earlier than you suspected.'

Krystiana felt her heart miss a beat. Matteo? King? That was *very* different from just having a romance with a prince.

Matteo frowned. 'What? No. You're as fit as a fiddle.'

'That's just it, Matteo. I'm *not*. I wish I were— I do. I know you need more time to get used to the idea, but you've had a whole lifetime waiting for this day. I'd hoped that a grand tour of Tamoura would be a gradual introduction to your new duties, but I'm having to face facts. My heart has given me a second warning now. If I want to be around to see this beautiful little one grow up and walk down the aisle one day, then I've got to take a step back earlier than I expected.'

Matteo glanced at Krystiana. 'What does that mean?'

'I'm going to abdicate *now*. The press have been notified already, and told that it's my recommendation that you are crowned as soon as it is possible.'

Matteo shook his head. 'Papà, *no!*'

Alberto reached out to take his hand. 'Matteo... No one *ever* feels ready. Do you think I was? Do you think I knew what I was doing when the crown was placed on my head? No. But it's how you act when it is. How you learn and grow to become the man you need to be to carry the country forward.'

'But...'

Matteo seemed lost for words, and almost on the verge of having to sit down. Instead he reached out for Krystiana's hand and squeezed it, not noticing the King's raised eyebrows as he did so, nor his questioning look at Krystiana.

'You still have months left before you said you'd abdicate. Take that time—a final farewell to the people. I—'

Alberto held up his hand for silence, his face stony. 'I was a new father when I took the throne. You were three weeks old. I was sleep-deprived, stressed and worn out. I'd just finished a world tour, had a new baby son... Life *happens*, Matteo. There will never be a perfect time. Dr Szenac, *you* seem to know my son well. You think he's ready, do you not?'

Krystiana swallowed, her mouth suddenly dry. She looked at Matteo, knowing he wanted her to say something that would support Alberto's carrying on for a bit longer. But she couldn't. She had to answer the King honestly.

'He's more than ready.'

Alberto smiled. 'You see? Everyone else knows you can do it.'

Matteo would make a great king. He was kind and caring, considerate and thoughtful. Yes, he had been through a great ordeal, but it had only served to make him stronger. More resolute.

But what did that mean for *them*? She had *slept* with him!

Alberto smiled. 'You will take the throne, Matteo.'

She saw Matteo glance at her with uncertainty, and in that glance so many things were conveyed. Doubt. Fear. Hesitation.

They were at the beginning of a relationship that could be something amazing. But she had no idea of how it was to be with someone like him! He was a *prince*. About to become a *king*. And she was just a normal girl from Poland. A doctor.

This acceleration of events was terrifying. What *was* she to him? Would it become serious? Was it casual? Would she be discarded and left behind?

* * *

'Are we going to talk about what happened today?' Matteo threw his jacket to one side as he walked into his quarters, Krystiana following slowly behind.

'Okay…'

'My father wants me to become King! I thought I had more time. I thought that…' he turned to look at her, saw the concern on her face '…that *we* had time.'

'We do. Don't we?'

'If my father has already alerted the press, then the focus of the whole country will be upon me. And also on *you*.'

She remembered what media attention felt like. It had been awful. Terrifying at times. But she had survived it. 'They would only be focused on me if we were together.'

He stopped pacing to face her. 'I guess that's the big question, isn't it?'

She gave a single nod. 'It is. What *am* I to you, Matteo?'

It was a terrifying question to ask. It would put him on the spot. But it was an answer she needed to hear, because she needed to know. Needed to prepare herself for whatever onslaught was coming.

'Honestly? I don't know.'

That wasn't good. A small part of her had

wanted him to say she was his everything. That he couldn't get enough of her. That he couldn't bear to be without her. But he wasn't saying any of those things.

'I don't want to hurt you. I know that. This situation is complex and extreme, and I can't assume that you'd want to be a part of this mad world that I live in.'

She said nothing. No, she didn't want to be hurt either. But she had a feeling she would be.

Krystiana sank down into a chair. 'Perhaps us being together is a bad idea? I get the feeling your father would not approve.'

Matteo looked down and away, as if he was weary.

'You're going to become *King*, Matteo. Sooner than you thought. Perhaps you and I ought to back off from one another for a while until all of that is done?'

Part of her thought that if they did back away from one another they would each have breathing space. This all seemed to be moving so fast! He was going to wear the crown! Perhaps with time apart he would begin to see that they weren't best suited, and by then she would have prepared herself for the inevitable and her heart would not be as broken as she suspected it might be.

Matteo sighed. 'You might be right.'

She'd suggested it, but it was still a shock that

he accepted it so readily. Perhaps he'd meant more to her than she to him?

Krystiana swallowed, her mouth dry, trying her hardest to stop the tears from burning the backs of her eyes, trying to be brave. They'd had one great night and it had been the most amazing night of her life. And to wake this morning, in his arms... She couldn't remember ever feeling so happy. But she'd always suspected that if they were to have any type of relationship it would be a brief one, and now it was looking more than likely that that was true.

It didn't make it any easier to know that he could happily discard her so quickly.

After Krystiana had gone Matteo stepped out onto his sun terrace and looked out over the hillsides. He knew he had to give them both space, but in his heart of hearts he also knew that, if he was being honest, nothing could ever have come from their relationship. He'd been an absolute fool to allow his desire and his lust for her to overcome every iota of common sense and logic he possessed!

His father had announced to the press that he was abdicating and that his son would be crowned King as soon as it was possible. The media was in a frenzy, as was to be expected, and he... He was apprehensive.

He should be thinking of his country. How the small kingdom of Isla Tamoura needed him to be a strong leader. And yet all he could think of was Krystiana.

Things had happened between them so quickly. And he suspected he knew why. They could both connect on something that not many people got to experience—thankfully. Their kidnapping. He couldn't imagine what it must have been like to have been taken by her own father. He tried to imagine his father doing such a thing. Locking him into a hole in the ground. His mind just couldn't compute it. Krystiana's father must have been so desperate after he lost his custody battle… He knew how crazy *he'd* almost gone, thinking he would never see his own child.

Krystiana had told him, hadn't she? That she didn't want a proper relationship. That she couldn't foresee having one. So really maybe he was doing her a favour? She didn't want this either!

His pathetic attempt to convince himself that he was doing this for *her* made him feel slightly ill.

He got up and began to pace once again—back and forth, back and forth. He caught a glimpse of his reflection in the mirror and stopped to stare at himself, trying to work out when it was that he had changed from being a man determined never to get involved with anyone again into a man who had barely been able to keep his emotions and desires in check around Krystiana.

He'd never wanted to feel loss again and yet he'd got involved with a woman he knew he could never have!

How on earth had he ever allowed it to happen?

She found herself standing outside Mara's office, holding the grey dress she'd borrowed draped over one arm. She knocked.

Mara opened her door. 'Krystiana! Come on in!' She stepped back to allow her entrance.

'I thought I'd better bring back your dress. It's been cleaned. I think one of the servants spirited it away when I was at the hospital this morning.'

Mara smiled, taking the dress from her. 'Thank you. But you could have kept it, you know?'

Krystiana shook her head. 'Oh, no! It must have cost a fortune. I couldn't do that.'

Mara gazed at her for a moment, obviously sensing her nerves and anxiety. 'What's wrong? Come on—sit down. Tell me what's going on.'

And suddenly the tears were falling. She couldn't help it. It was almost as if Mara's empathy and kindness had just opened up the dam and it had all come pouring out.

Mara, bless her, sat next to her with an arm around her shoulders. Just being there. Just waiting for when she was ready to talk.

'Matteo and I…' Krystiana sniffed, dabbing at her eyes with the tissue that Mara offered her. 'We've been…er…' How to say it? This was his ex-wife! But she was also his best friend, so…

'You've been…courting?'

She knew? 'Not really. Not *dating*, as such. Just… I'm not sure how it happened, really, but…'

Mara waited.

'We slept together.' She felt awful telling Mara this.

'And now it's complicated?'

Krystiana nodded. 'It always was.'

'I understand. Matteo and I, even though we knew our future, were caught up in an extraordinary situation. And now the man that you…you have feelings for is about to be King, and that's not a normal thing at all for anyone to have to face.'

'No one would approve of us.'

'You don't know that.'

Krystiana didn't have to think for too long. 'I do. Matteo held my hand in front of his father and I could see he wasn't pleased about it.'

'The world is complicated, Krystiana. Nothing is always simple or as it seems. Sometimes all you can do is go with what your heart tells you.'

'It's telling me so many things.'

'Then perhaps you should ask it a question? How would you feel never to have Matteo in your life ever again?'

She couldn't imagine what that would be like. To only see him on the television… In the news-papers… Online… 'It would be awful.'

Mara smiled. 'But you would survive it?'

'I've already survived so much. Had my heart broken too many times. I'm not sure I want to go through that again.'

'Sometimes we have no choice about our bat-tles.'

Krystiana smiled ruefully. 'You sound like you're trying to tell me to prepare myself. That there is no future for us.'

Mara looked away. 'I like you, Krystiana. I think you and Matteo could be amazing together. You'd make each other happy.'

'But…?'

'But if you want to be with him then you need to talk to him.'

'About what?'

Mara smiled. 'About everything.'

CHAPTER ELEVEN

MATTEO OPENED THE door to his quarters to see Krystiana standing there, looking apprehensive and nervous. Smiling, he welcomed her in, dropping a kiss on her cheek. She looked so beautiful, her eyes bright and kind, her smile full and wide. He felt his heart lift at seeing her, even though he felt depressed.

'Hi,' he said.

'Hi. I wonder if you have a minute to talk?'

'Sure. Can I get you a drink?'

'No, it's all right. I just want to say this whilst I have the nerve to and then I'll go.'

Oh. That didn't sound good. But, then again, she was smiling—so what did that mean? Had she made a decision?

'I'm all ears.'

'*Yes.*'

He narrowed his eyes. 'Yes…?'

She laughed. 'Yes! To you. To *us*. One of us has to say it! I want us to try to be together. Despite all that's going on, despite you becoming King, and despite other people's disapproval— when there is any, which I'm expecting there to be. I'm just a doctor, after all, and—'

'Hang on—let me get this straight. You want us to be a…a couple?'

His heart soared. Not for one moment had he thought she would come to such a conclusion, but she had, and it was wonderful, and despite all his fears he wanted this one moment when he did something for *him*. Because his life was about to spiral madly out of control when he became King. He knew he was throwing caution to the wind, despite the rules, but surely he could worry about those at a later time?

'Come here.' He pulled her into his arms, his lips meeting hers, and he kissed her as he'd never kissed her before!

He knew what this had cost her. He knew how terrified she must have been to say it. And it felt *so right*. This was the woman he'd been waiting for his entire life. She was perfect. Intelligent, kind, loving, beautiful. And she understood him. Understood more than anyone else ever could. Because she'd been through it, too.

And when his father had collapsed he'd felt *safe*, knowing she was with him. He'd felt loved, knowing that she was thinking about *him*, that he was thinking about *her*.

She was his strength. His heart. His life. And though he was worried about what the future might entail for them, his fear was not as strong as his love. His need. That was a bridge they could cross later. Surely there was a way?

'I love you so much, Krystiana Szenac!'

She smiled back. 'And I love *you*!'

They kissed. Unable to get enough of each other. He had no doubt that he would have taken her to his bed right there and then, if he'd been able to, but he had people coming. Delegates. Business meetings.

'Let's celebrate! Just you and me. Away from here. I could get us reservations at Jacaranda. Very discreet.'

'Go out with you in public?' Her face was flushed with excitement and nerves and apprehension.

He nodded. 'We need to get away from this place. Just be *us*.'

Krystiana nodded and gave him a quick kiss before she headed back to the door. 'Dress code?'

He gave it some thought. 'You'd look beautiful in anything.'

She laughed. '*Formal* would have done nicely.'

'Formal, it is.'

'Right. Then I'm off to get ready.'

He checked his watch. 'It's two-thirty in the afternoon.'

'A girl needs time to look her best, Matteo.'

'You're already perfect.'

She smiled and blew him a kiss. 'Good answer. But I'm still going to have a bath and do my hair.'

She began to close the doors behind her.

'Wait!' he called, sliding over to the door in his socks, skidding to a halt in front of her. 'One last kiss?'

She pressed her mouth to his and he savoured the taste of her.

'Not the last, Matteo. But the first of *many*.'

She'd needed to be brave many times in her life, but going to see Matteo and admitting what she wanted, to be in a relationship with him, was probably one of the bravest things she had ever done. She had put herself *out there*. As if she was on a precipice and he had the ability to knock her off, to send her crashing to her doom.

She'd given him that power and he hadn't let her down at all. Her gut instinct had been *right*! He wanted to be with her as much as she wanted to be with him!

And she was quickly learning that one of the advantages of living in a palace was that there seemed to be a hairdresser, stylist and make-up artist always on site. Apparently Giulia was there mostly for Mara and Alex's sake, but she was thrilled to get her hands on someone new and decide what to do with her.

'Your hair is just *bellissimo*! Thick and long.' Giulia was running her fingers through it, admiring it, trying it this way, then that. 'I think we need a messy up-do. Like this—see? But if we leave these strands here and here we can make tiny plaits and twist them through…like this. *Si?*'

Krystiana had never done more than put her hair in a thick plait. 'Whatever you think is right will be fine.'

'We can tousle it, tease it, and if we are careful we can use jewelled slides here and there. Let me do it and I'll show you—I promise you'll love it.'

'Okay.'

'And what were you thinking for make-up?' Giulia looked at her carefully in the mirror. 'Such expressive eyes… You need more than mascara on those. How about a deep, dark smoky eye? A nude lip? Earrings to match the jewels in your hair?'

Krystiana frowned. 'You're the expert. How long will all that take?'

'A couple of hours. We have plenty of time and then we can take a look at your wardrobe.'

'My wardrobe…?'

She didn't really have much in there. It wasn't as if she had loads to choose from. She'd mostly got ordinary work clothes with her. Suits…

Dresses fit for being in her practice office—not a romantic soirée.

'Some things have been sent over for you.'

She turned in her seat. 'Oh? From whom?'

'The Crown Prince.'

'Matteo?'

'Well, he had a little help from me. I went shopping at his request.'

'When?'

'When you first arrived at the palace. He wasn't sure how much we would be able to rescue from your home, so he sent me out to fetch you a range of outfits.'

'Oh. But you don't know my sizes.'

'Stylists can *tell*. Just by looking. Trust me—I have picked you out some wonderful things.'

Krystiana smiled at her reflection as Giulia set to work with her hair. She quite liked it that he'd wanted to get some clothes for her, and she wasn't at all upset that he might have been a bit presumptuous in assuming that she was staying.

If he hadn't done it then she'd be knocking on Mara's door again, raiding *her* wardrobe! And there was something wrong about wearing the clothes of a man's ex-wife to make him fall for her! She was looking forward to searching through the boxes and bags that were now on the bed to see what there was.

She'd never been treated in such a way! Had

always been careful with money, even though her job paid well. Growing up in a household where her mother had scrimped and saved every *zloty* had clearly rubbed off on her.

With her hair looking exquisite and her face made up by the talented Giulia, who could do things with a blender brush that Krystiana had no idea how to replicate, she set to going through the new outfits.

There were trouser suits and tailored dresses, flowing skirts and perfect heels. Linen trousers…even a couple of swimsuits! But in the end they both agreed that a duck-egg-blue dress, that skimmed over her hips and flared out just above the knee would be perfect.

Krystiana tried it on, twirling and twisting in front of the full-length mirror to check how it looked. 'This is so pretty, Giulia! Did you choose it?'

'Matteo chose this one. He said it would match your eyes and it does.'

Krystiana smiled. 'Good. Then I shall definitely wear it. Are we all done?'

Giulia tapped her lips as she assessed her. 'It needs one more thing… Here.' And she pulled from one of the bags a small box, cracking it open for Krystiana to see the jewelled bracelet inside.

It glittered and caught the light and it was the

most beautiful thing she had ever seen. 'Oh, my word! He bought me *that*?'

'Yes.'

'It must have cost a fortune! I can't wear that! I'll be afraid of losing it all night.'

'It has a safety chain. Try it.'

Giulia clipped it around her wrist and she felt the weight of it on her arm. Just enough to notice. If it *did* fall off she would know instantly.

'So… I'm ready?'

'Yes, you are. I'll gather my things together and then I'll go.'

'Thank you, Giulia. You're a miracle-worker!'

'It was my pleasure. Have a good night.'

There was a gentle knock at her door and Krystiana opened it.

Matteo stood there, looking handsome in a smart suit, his white shirt crisp and clean, open at the collar. He looked like a handsome spy, set to seduce.

'You look…' He looked her up and down, his eyes appreciative. 'Amazing!'

She blushed. 'Thank you! So do you.'

'May I escort you down to the car?'

He held out his arm and she slipped hers through it, smiling. 'Thank you! You may.'

Together they walked through the palace corridors, past various members of staff going about their duties. They all looked up and smiled at the two of them and Krystiana felt admired and adored. Clearly they were a handsome couple.

In the car, they were driven slowly through the grounds of the palace and out through the gates, then down towards the bustling capital city of Ventura. Before she knew it they were pulling up outside a smart restaurant, set back from the road. Either side of the doors were railings behind which had gathered a bunch of people with cameras.

She felt her heart begin to race. 'Are they paparazzi?'

'Looks like it.'

'How did they know we were coming here?'

'I don't know. Someone must have let something slip. Shall we go back? We don't have to go out there.'

Her heart was racing and she felt a little clammy. Back in the palace she'd been sheltered from this, and though she knew she'd agreed to this, now that the moment was here it still felt a little...frightening.

'Just stay by my side—all right?' she said.

He nodded. 'Keep your eyes on me. When we're out of the vehicle we'll give them one moment when we stand together, give a quick smile, and then we'll be indoors. I promise you they can't see inside, and they can't step through the door. We'll have privacy for our meal. All right?'

She nodded, not sure she could speak.

'Okay. Deep breath and then one, two, three...'

Matteo opened the car door and suddenly a barrage of flashing lights assaulted her, blinding her slightly. She could hear clicks and whirrs and felt the flashes blinding her, leaving imprints on her retinas. She had to fight the urge to hold her hand in front of her face and run inside.

Instead, she gripped his arm, feeding on his sure strength and composure, and when she looked up at him he was smiling down at her with such ease that she couldn't help but smile back. And then they gave the press what they wanted. A quick pose. A quick smile. A small wave and then they were inside the restaurant.

She let out a heavy breath and looked to Matteo with relief. He was smiling at her and he kissed her gently on the lips. 'You did great.'

'It all happened so fast.'

'We all learn how to work the press. Give them enough to keep them fed and watered, but always leave them hanging on for more. And always be polite.'

'It almost feels like a game.'

'It is. They're all in competition with one another for the best shot, the best photo, the best smile. Because that's what sells.'

'I guess tomorrow everyone will know who I am?'

He nodded. 'They won't know for sure, though. It will all be speculation.'

So he can deny us later?

She hated it that the thought flittered through her brain, and she dismissed it. If he'd not wanted anyone to know about them then he would have ordered the driver to bring them here. He wouldn't have got out of the car with her. She was just being ridiculous and nervous because she was putting herself out there, on the line. Of course she could trust him.

The maître d' met them and escorted them to a small private booth at the back of the restaurant. A piano played softly in the background, and she quickly realised it wasn't being piped through speakers but was an actual pianist sitting at the instrument.

Candles lit the restaurant, alongside wall sconces and chandeliers, creating an intimate mood, and she sat at the table, suddenly feeling hungry. The nerves from facing the press had emptied her stomach.

A server draped her serviette over her lap and poured water into their glasses. 'Would you like to see the menu?'

'Thank you,' she said.

The server bowed and presented them each with a leather-bound menu. 'The special today is venison, which has been marinated in juniper, served with a parsnip *velouté* and a wild mushroom sauce.'

'Thank you,' she said again, and smiled shyly at the server and watched him walk away. 'This place is beautiful.'

'It's a favourite of mine. The chef is very good.'

She smiled. 'Did you come here with Mara?' she asked. She didn't want to think that this was where Matteo had brought *all* the women he'd wanted to impress in his past.

'No. I didn't. I only found this place after Mara and I had split.'

She smiled shyly. Thankful.

'So, what do you fancy?'

Krystiana beamed and reached across the table to take his hand. 'You.'

'Tell me what you were like as a little boy.'

She couldn't imagine what he must have been like. *Her* only recollections of growing up in Poland seemed to be around her own kidnapping, and then afterwards moving to Isla Tamoura. Adapting to a new way of life and thinking how strange it was. Surely his childhood had been a lot more sturdy.

He smiled. 'My father would tell you that I got into all types of mischief.'

'And what would *you* tell me?'

Matteo laughed. 'That he was right! There was this one time he was having an official meeting. Very important. Children not allowed. I can remember being fascinated about why all these important-looking people were allowed into this room and I wasn't! Was there some treasure there they were all looking at? Were they eating fabulous food? Did they have great computer games? I felt sure I was missing out on something, so I crept in and hid behind a drape at the back of my father's chair. I listened and listened, absolutely sure that I'd hear something secret or amazing. But they were droning on about olive yields and crop rotations and it was the most boring thing I'd ever heard—so I thought I'd liven things up.'

'What did you do?'

'I jumped out from behind the curtain and made the loudest and best dinosaur noise that I could possibly make.'

She laughed, imagining it. 'What happened?'

'My father turned in his seat and gave me *"the look"*. I knew then I was in trouble. I was escorted out, and about an hour later he came and told me off—said that as punishment I had to help the gardener for the afternoon.'

'Wow.'

'And of course you know how *that* turned out. I ended up designing nearly all of it.'

'It sounds like you were a very happy young boy.'

'I was. I *was* lucky.' He looked at her. 'How about you? There must be something from your childhood that's a good memory?'

She had to think about it. But then she remembered. 'My father once promised me a pony. He said that one day that I would have the best pony in the world! He got me a poster for my room, and a small cuddly toy that was a horse, but he said that one day I'd ride a pony that was all mine. I never got to do it, but I remember how hard he tried to give me what I wanted. He wasn't always a bad man.'

'Matilde could be yours.'

She looked at him. Was he serious? 'What…?'

'She could! You on Matilde, myself on Galileo—we could have many happy rides together.'

'You see a future for us, then?' she asked, her heart beating merrily. She was testing him gently. Needing the reassurance of his words.

He sipped his water. 'Of course.'

Later, Matteo walked her back to her rooms in the palace. Once inside the doors of his family home she had pulled off her heels, and she padded barefoot through the corridors, her head leaning against his arm.

She'd had such a wonderful evening with him. Listening to his stories and tales, laughing at his anecdotes, of which he had many, and just enjoying listening to him speak.

She realised just how long it had been since she'd been able to do that. Her whole adult life had been filled with patients—sitting and listening, assessing, analysing, looking for clues to their physical or mental state, considering diagnoses, selecting help methods and suggesting therapies and strategies they could use to get better.

But tonight she had just *enjoyed*. And she had told him a few tales of her own. Not having to be guarded about what she said, knowing that he would enjoy whatever it was and really listen to it.

She'd felt so good with him. So natural. And as she'd looked into his eyes over the table, as they'd eaten delicious food that had tasted as good as it looked, she'd just known that she could fall for this man hugely. If she hadn't already.

At her door, she turned to face him, pulling him towards her for a kiss. His lips on hers felt magical. This truly was blissful! To have such joy and happiness after all that they had both gone through. It almost felt as if it were a dream. And to think she had nearly denied herself such happiness…

'I want you to stay with me tonight,' she said boldly, looking deep into his eyes, telling him with her gaze exactly what she wanted.

He kissed her again, and then she took his hand and led him inside…

* * *

'Could you undo the zip?'

Krystiana turned away from him, to present him with her back. He gazed at the soft slope of her shoulders, at the gentle curls of honey hair at the nape of her neck and at the long zip that trailed the length of her spine. He took hold of the zipper and slowly lowered it, leaning in to kiss her soft skin as he did so.

She leaned back against him, gasping softly as his lips trailed feather touches and his hands slipped under the dress at each shoulder and slid the fabric to the floor.

Turning again, she faced him with a smile and he took in everything about her. The softness of her skin, the gentle swell of her breasts, her narrow waist, the feminine curve of her lips.

'You're so beautiful,' he whispered, reaching for her mouth with his own, sliding his hands down her sides, curving them over her buttocks and pulling her against him. Against his hardness. Wanting her to know how much he wanted her.

'Matteo!' She gasped his name as his hands cupped her breasts, and then again as his tongue found her nipples, delicately licking and teasing each tip. He worked lower, down to her belly, hooking his thumbs under her panties and slowly, slowly pulling them down.

He wanted to lose himself in her, but a loud voice in the back of his mind was yelling at him, telling him that this was *wrong*. That nothing could come of it. He would have to let her go and he was being a terrible man—keeping up the façade that everything was fine. Soon he would have to tell her the truth, and that would tear her apart. He didn't want to be just another man who would break her heart, so he kept putting it off and putting it off—and now look at where they were.

She thought they were making love.

But he knew he was saying goodbye.

She woke in his arms. A lazy smile was upon her face. Her body was still tingling, comforted by the feel of Matteo spooning her from behind.

Last night had been everything she had ever dreamed of, and she knew that out in the wider world the people of Isla Tamoura would be waking up to newspaper reports of the coronation and the Crown Prince's new beau. They would have the rest of their lives to enjoy each other. They'd made it official last night, with that public appearance. Now everyone would know.

Briefly she wondered if she ought to call the practice and make arrangements for her patients to be taken on by Dr Bonetti for a short while. Later on she could decide about when she'd return. It had been so long since she'd taken any time off she felt sure Dr Bonetti wouldn't mind, and she'd just covered for him, so...

There's plenty of time before I have to do that, though.

Getting out of bed, she pulled on her robe and opened up the double doors that led outside, closing her eyes to the wonderful warmth of the early-morning sun.

This would be her life from now on. This wonder. This joy. Living in the palace with the man of her dreams, the love of her life. Yes, she knew she loved him. Everything would be different now.

She glanced back at Matteo, still blissfully asleep in her bed, his face relaxed, and realised they'd both got through the night without a nightlight. It was as if the love they had between them was what they needed to be strong enough to fight off the fears that plagued them.

Was that all it took? A loving pair of arms?

Whatever it was, she didn't mind. She was happy. And in love. Probably for the first time in her life. She had fallen for him deeply.

His eyes blinked open and as soon as he saw her he smiled. *'Buongiorno.'*

'Buongiorno.'

'You're up already.'

'Ready to face the world!'

He groaned. 'No. Not yet. Let's just stay here and pretend the rest of the world doesn't exist. Come back to bed.'

She smiled coyly at him and padded back towards him, disrobing and falling into his arms, feeling his lips on hers and delightful sensations rippling through her once again.

'Aren't you tired?'

'Of this? *Never.*'

Krystiana laughed. 'Don't you have to go to the hospital this morning?'

Matteo groaned and rolled over to check his watch, blinking at the time. 'Yes. Of course. You're right. Five minutes…then I'll get dressed.'

'Five minutes?' She bit her lip and looked at him questioningly.

He laughed, unable to help himself. 'I can do a lot in five minutes.'

And then he disappeared under the bed sheet and she felt his mouth trail down her skin, lower and lower, until she gasped with surprise and delight.

She'd wanted to capture the moment of Alex playing in Matteo's beloved flower garden. She'd thought it would be a wonderful gift for him. So as Alex frolicked amongst the blooms, trying to catch butterflies with a gauzy net, Krystiana stood back, splashing colour onto canvas.

She'd show him when he got back from seeing his father! He would love it. It would be unique. It would be put in pride of place in his quarters. The lush greens of all the foliage, the spots of gold, bronze, cherry-red, fuchsia-pink and lapis-blue flowers, and amongst it all a beautiful little girl, her long ebony locks flowing behind her, her net held high, ready to swoop.

'Look at me, Krissy—look!'

She was so beautiful, Matteo's daughter, and it was important to Krystiana that they got along. She wanted to create a happy painting. Made with love.

Just as she was adding the finishing touches she felt a prickle on the back of her neck. The sensation of being watched.

She turned to see who it might be.

It was Matteo. Up on his sun terrace, looking down at them. He was far enough away not to be able to see the painting, but there was something about his stance that made her think he was upset.

She put down her brushes and wiped her hands on a soft cloth. 'Alex? Let the painting dry, won't you? Don't touch it. I'm just going to see if your father is all right.'

Her first thought was that maybe something had happened with his father. Had King Alberto deteriorated? Perhaps he'd had a heart attack in the night?

Oh, please don't let him be dead!

She hated to think of Matteo being hurt in such a way. Going through the loss of his last remaining parent...

The thought made her steps slow, and for a moment she stopped still completely, just to breathe. To gather herself—strengthen herself for whatever revelation was about to come. It had to be something bad, didn't it? Otherwise Matteo would have come down to see her in the gardens with Alex.

Everything had been going so well since last night. They'd both finally found happiness. Was the beginning of their love going to be marred by death? She sincerely hoped not...

Krystiana didn't knock as she entered his quarters. She knew he would still be out on the sun terrace and he was—standing with his back to her, ramrod-straight. There was a sternness to the set of his shoulders, to the upright nature of his posture—as if he was holding himself so as not to break.

'Matteo?'

He didn't answer her. Or turn around. And that alarmed her. She walked to his side so that she could see his face. It was cold and stony. Like a statue.

She reached out to touch his hand with hers. 'Matteo? Are you all right? What's happened?'

He said nothing for a while, then he blinked and squeezed her fingers tightly, before responding, 'I went to see my father.'

She felt as if a cold, dead lump was weighting down her stomach. 'Is he all right?'

'Fine. Well, health-wise, he is. The doctors think he can come home.'

She felt a wave of relief surge over her. 'But that's *great* news!'

He nodded. 'It is.'

'So…why aren't you happy? You look… stressed.'

And that was when she noticed that in his other hand he held a small glass of whisky. He lifted it to his mouth and sank the drink in one gulp. Wasn't it a little early for hard liquor?

'Matteo? You're scaring me. Tell me what's going on. *Now.*'

He turned to look at her and she could see that he had been crying. His eyes were red and puffy.

'My father saw the newspapers this morning. He was not pleased that he had to learn about us through a third party.'

She sucked in a breath. 'Okay…' That was acceptable. They should apologise for that. King

Alberto should have been told by them. They'd got that bit wrong. 'Does he not like me?'

'He does. But…' He glanced at his glass and saw that it was empty. Scowling, he placed it down on the balcony edge. 'He reminded me of a certain unpalatable truth.'

She blinked, not understanding. 'What truth?'

Matteo turned away, as if unable to look her in the eyes. And that scared her.

'The law of my country states that those first in line to the throne can only marry another of royal blood.'

What? No. That couldn't be right!

But the more she thought about what that meant, the more she knew something like this had always been going to happen. It had all been going too well.

The tears escaped. Trickling down her cheeks. 'Royal blood?'

He could only marry a princess? Or a duchess? Something like that? Well, she wasn't either of those things! She was just a girl from Poland who'd once lived in a giant block of flats. A girl from a poor family whose father had hunted rabbit and pigeon to feed his family meat. A girl who had fled to this island seeking a better life than the one she'd had to leave behind.

They were worlds apart. The only way she'd

have royal blood would be if she stole it from someone and kept it in a small vial!

'This is ridiculous! It's got to be wrong!'

'It's not wrong. It's an archaic law of my land and has been for hundreds of years.'

Her eyes widened as her brain scrambled to find some way out of this. 'But if we didn't know, surely it isn't our fault?'

He turned and walked over to the liquor cabinet. Without a word he refilled his glass and knocked back the whisky again, his gaze downcast to the floor.

And suddenly she knew. She tried to make him look at her. 'You *did* know. You knew and yet you slept with me anyway. You made me think that we could be together! How could you? How could you treat me like this? Like a...a plaything. A toy! What did you think I was? Some kind of casual fling?'

'Krystiana—'

But she didn't want to hear it. She'd told him she'd been hurt before, and how much it would cost her to trust someone again, and what had he done? He'd lied. He'd kept secrets. He'd used her. For his own gratification!

He was worse than Adamo.

Overcome with tears and humiliation, she fled from his room.

* * *

Matteo winced as his door slammed behind her and felt sick to his stomach. The visit with his father had been a lost battle before he'd even entered the room—and now this. Surely there must have been another way he could have done this? Another way he could have gently explained how they could never be more than what they were now.

But his father had forced his hand. He had told him that he needed to tell her the truth or that he, Alberto himself, would have the royal chamberlain inform her of the rules by the end of the day. Tell her that she would have to give up her claim on the King's son because he could never be hers.

'Why are you doing this?' he'd asked his father.

'I'm trying to stop it before either of you get hurt.'

But it was already too late. His father didn't know the depth of his feelings for Krystiana. Or hers for him. And he hated it that he had trampled all over her heart with his dirty shoes.

But, hell, she'd not wanted a relationship either—so what the hell was *she* doing, allowing them to get into such a situation? He'd thought they'd both be safe. Neither of them had wanted it and yet somehow, in some way, they had been unable to stay away from each other.

And now he was faced with another loss. Another heartbreak. Was he doomed to suffer? He should never have got involved, he told himself once again, as he slammed his hand against the wall in frustration and upset, and he would never allow himself to get into a situation like this ever again.

His heart would be off-limits.

Access granted only to his daughter.

Krystiana refused to pack the clothes that had been bought for her. Or the jewellery. Or any of the gifts she'd been given during her time in the palace. If she took any of it all it would do, when she got home, would be to remind her of what might have been, and her heart was instinctively telling her that if she wanted to get over this then she had to leave it all behind. Then she could almost pretend that it had never happened. Like she had when she'd left Krakow. All she'd taken with her then had been some clothes in a small suitcase and a solitary doll with only one arm.

She'd seen plenty of patients in her time who had used denial as an effective tool to pretend that bad stuff hadn't happened. And right now she thought it was a damned good strategy! Though she'd suggested that they might do better by facing the bad stuff, so that they could heal, right now she wanted to wholeheartedly embrace the concept.

Angrily she went from drawer to drawer, grabbing her clothes roughly and shoving them into her suitcase, throwing in her shoes. She didn't even bother to wrap her paints and spare canvases separately.

Who cares if I get paint over everything?

She didn't. Her heart had been broken the instant she'd realised that Matteo had lied to her, and she knew she couldn't stay a moment longer. She couldn't believe the mess she had got herself into!

I fought against this attraction. I should have listened to myself.

If she had, then none of this would have happened and she'd already be out of here. She should never have stayed for that ball. She should have gone.

But it had been impossible. Her desire for him had been plain fact. There'd been no way to walk away from her love. Her soul mate. The man she'd seen herself with all the way into the future.

How gullible she must have seemed for him to use her like that, knowing how she'd been treated in the past. He'd known what it had taken for her to open to him like that, to put herself out there, and he'd—

She cried out loud as pain ripped through her chest and hiccupped her way through her final packing. Bruno sat in the corner, his head tilted as he watched her frantic movements, trying to work out what was going on.

His father must have delighted in forcing Matteo to tell her the truth. Or perhaps she should *thank* the King? She'd seen it in his face, that time Matteo had clutched Krystiana's hand for support in the hospital. The way his eyes had narrowed... She should have questioned it then.

Behind her, the doors to her apartment opened.

'You're leaving?'

Mara stared at her, her face a mask of shock and concern.

Krystiana wiped at her eyes, determined to stop crying once and for all! 'I have no choice!'

'There must be something you can do...'

'There isn't, so...' She turned to Mara and pulled her towards her for a hug. 'Thank you for being my friend here. It could have been awkward between us, but you made it so easy. Thank you.'

Mara hugged her back. 'Are you kidding me? It's so obvious that what you and Matteo have is real. You look at each other the way Philippe and I do.'

Krystiana sniffed. 'It was never real. Matteo *knew* I couldn't be with him.'

Mara looked away.

Krystiana stared at her. 'You did too?' she asked with incredulity.

'I'm sorry. But I couldn't be the one to tell you. To break your heart.'

Krystiana slammed down the clips on her suitcase. 'A heads-up might have been nice!'

'I tried! I told you to talk to him!'

But she didn't want to hear any more. Did *everyone* lie? 'I've got to go. Say goodbye to Alex for me?'

'Where are you going?'

She shrugged. 'A hotel somewhere? A bed and breakfast?' She looked at Bruno. 'One that takes dogs…'

'Will I ever see you again?'

'Do you read the *Lancet*?' Krystiana smiled, trying to crack a joke in the midst of her trauma.

'No.'

'Then I guess not.'

'I'll talk to Matteo.'

'There's no point. I wouldn't have any more to do with him if he was the last man alive.'

'Krystiana, please! Promise me you'll wait here until I get back?'

She nodded, knowing she was going to break her promise. But what did she owe Mara, if anything'? Mara had been complicit in this lie, too. Mara whom she'd thought was a friend.

After Matteo's ex-wife had left Krystiana took one last look around the place and then left, trailing her little suitcase behind her.

'Come on, Bruno. Let's go.'

CHAPTER TWELVE

SHE'D NOT BEEN lying when she'd told Mara she'd stay at a hotel or a bed and breakfast. She just hadn't said it would be in Rome.

Isla Tamoura was not a place she could be right now. Everyone would know her—know her face. She wouldn't be able to find refuge at work either. People would show up just to gawp at her and ask questions. To see the royal fool. She needed to go somewhere no one would find her.

She'd dropped Bruno off at her aunt's place. Thankfully she'd been out, so she'd left her aunt a note on the counter. Bruno would be fine with her—she knew that.

At the airport, the first thing she spotted was her face on the front of a newspaper. She was standing next to Matteo outside the restaurant last night. Smiling. Looking nervous, but happy.

Feeling sick, she fumbled in her handbag for a pair of large sunglasses and let her long hair down loose. She didn't want anyone spotting her. Didn't want anyone recognising who she was.

She sneaked into the women's toilet and splashed her face with cold water, staring at her reflection, trying to equate the drawn-looking woman in the mirror with the one who had just this very morning woken up in the arms of the man she loved. A woman who had believed that her worst problem at the time was whether she'd have time for a quick shower before breakfast.

How was she here? Why had he lied? When he knew that the truth was the most important thing he could have told her?

Sliding the sunglasses back onto her face, she headed out of the bathroom and went to the customer service desk.

'Are there any flights to Rome soon?' she asked the perfectly groomed woman behind the desk.

The woman, whose name tag read *Leonora*, tapped at her keyboard, reading the screen in front of her. 'Yes, ma'am, there's a flight at three this afternoon.'

'Any seats available?'

'Yes, ma'am. Window and aisle.'

'Okay. Who do I need to see to book that?'

Leonora told her where to go, and before she knew it Krystiana had a plane ticket and had checked her luggage. Only an hour until her flight time. What to do to pass the time?

She saw a coffee shop and felt the need for a huge slug of caffeine, and maybe some restorative chocolate, despite the feeling in her stomach.

She sat down at a small table, trying not to be noticed. Opposite her, a man sat with a woman whom she supposed to be his wife. They were discussing her picture on the front page of the newspaper. Wondering whether they were serious? Whether they were in love?

She tried to sink down in her seat, hoping no one would notice her.

I should have bought a paper to hide behind.

She looked about her and saw a discarded one on the table next to her. She picked it up and shook it open, hiding her face from the crowds.

One hour to go and she could be out of here!

Matteo stared at the empty apartment. 'She's really gone.' He felt guilty. Angry. It had all come crashing down around his ears so quickly. Such intense happiness, contentment and love, and now this.

He was feeling empty. Stunned.

Heartbroken.

The thought that he might never see her again almost crushed him into inertia. It was like being back in that cave, wondering if he'd ever see his loved ones again?

Mara laid a friendly hand upon his arm, her face filled with sympathy. 'She told me she'd wait.'

'She didn't want to get involved with me. *Told* me she didn't want a relationship. That she didn't want to be that vulnerable.'

'She loved you, though. You can't help who you fall in love with.'

'Like you and Philippe?' It was a cheap shot, and it was out of his bitter mouth before he could reel it back in. He was hurting and wanted to lash out, but he should never have lashed out at his best friend. 'I'm sorry. Forget that.'

'No, you're right. I gave up on you. I left you behind.'

'You thought I was dead. It's hardly the same.'

'But I still must have hurt you.'

'I thought I'd never love again. I was determined that no one, anywhere, would open me up to loss. Ever.'

'Krystiana left because she couldn't be with you in the way that she needed.'

'She left because I *lied*. I hurt her. Whatever must she think of me?'

'She'll be okay. She's strong.'

'She shouldn't *have* to be okay. Shouldn't have to be strong. She deserved the truth, but I never told her any of it because I knew how deep I was already in!' He'd never felt so frustrated in all his life. 'I thought I could bury my head in the sand. I thought I could find a way around it.'

'I'm sorry, Matteo.'

'I need to speak with my father.'

'He's resting. He needs to take it easy. You can't go in there, all guns blazing.'

'So what do I do?'

'I don't know. Maybe you should just accept the fact that you got this wrong?'

Matteo sank onto the end of the bed. 'In the worst way possible...'

'You don't know that for sure.'

He looked at her with resignation. 'Yes, I do.'

On arrival in Rome, Krystiana headed straight to the nearest information desk and looked for hotel and bed and breakfast listings. She didn't want anywhere in the main city, but something on the periphery. Somewhere a bit more remote.

She found a perfect place called the Catalina that belonged to an elderly couple. Their bed and breakfast was on the outskirts of Rome, in Lazio, and her bedroom windows looked out over the countryside that formed part of the Riserva Naturale di Decima-Malafede. A nature reserve that was meant to host a population of wild boar.

After the hustle and bustle of life in the palace

and work in Ventura, it felt good to be looking out at trees and grassland. Anything that didn't remind her of life at the palace was absolutely fine by her.

She checked in under a made-up name, wearing the floppy sunhat she'd bought in duty-free and the large sunglasses that covered half her face. And then she sat in her room, dwelling on all that had passed.

Krystiana was doing what she always did in times of trauma—she was painting. Her room was beginning to fill with some pretty dark canvases now that she'd been here a week. It stank of paint and turpentine. She hadn't eaten much and seemed to be existing on coffee. Espresso.

She refused to do anything else. Hadn't turned on the television or read the news. She didn't want to hear anything about what might be happening on Isla Tamoura. Didn't want to think about Matteo in his garden, or playing with Alex, or eating breakfast on his sun terrace. To wonder whether he was being groomed to meet up with women who were more *suitable*. With *royal* blood. As opposed to the normal red stuff that ran in *her* veins.

He hadn't tried to contact her—which she was pleased about. It was what they both needed. No contact. Otherwise it might be too painful.

I've been a fool!

She'd spent her entire life telling herself that she was worth something. That she wasn't damaged goods and that she deserved the truth. And even though she'd thought she'd found it in Matteo, clearly she'd been wrong. He'd been forced to reveal his lies. The way Adamo had. Her mind reeled as to how she could have been so misled. She'd believed so much that he felt the same about her.

He was a good actor. Perhaps it was something they taught young royals on Isla Tamoura. Always to seem confident and believable. There were all those speeches they had to make—that had to be part of it, didn't it? Because being a good, strong king was something he wanted to present himself as. He was practised.

I never stood a chance.

And now, just as she'd known she couldn't dig her way out of that hole in the ground when she was six, she knew that the situation she was in was just as futile. It was almost a special skill she'd developed—acknowledging when something was a hopeless case—and there were only two things you could do when you had no power at all: accept it, or suffer trying to fight back.

She'd had enough suffering in her life. And though she knew it was going to hurt, walking away from the man she loved, she knew she had no choice. She was resigning herself to the fact that she'd been right. People were weak and they let you down. Love saved no one.

She hoped she would learn something from this experience. Learn that she could only ever depend upon herself, as she'd always suspected. That at the end of the day, no matter how many people you had around you, it was down to you and you alone to survive.

'What about Katherine? She seemed very interested in you.'

Alberto sat across the breakfast table from Matteo, who was nonchalantly tearing pastries apart, but only nibbling tiny parts of them.

He sighed. 'She was very nice. Clever conversation…'

'And *pretty*!' His father laughed. 'She would provide you with some beautiful children.'

Matteo smiled. 'I already have a beautiful child.'

'Your coronation is in one month. Are you going to be ascending the throne with a fiancée?'

'I don't think so, Papà. A relationship takes time to build. I can't make a decision like that after only spending one evening with someone.'

'Of course not. But it would be nice for the country to have another happy celebration to look forward to after the coronation.'

Was that all that mattered? All that *should* matter? His *country*? What of his own life? Did that not matter at all any more? 'I won't be marrying anyone, Papà. I dined with Katherine because she was a guest here. No other reason. Not because the country needs a pick-me-up. I've already sacrificed so much—don't ask me for any more.'

Alberto held up his hands in supplication. 'Fair enough. I won't push. Now, are you bringing me my granddaughter later today? I haven't seen Alexandra for an age.'

'She'll be here later. Mara is bringing her over with Philippe.'

'He's a good man for her.'

'Yes, he is. Better than I ever was.'

His father looked at him, considering him. 'And…the doctor? You haven't heard from her?'

'No.'

Matteo did his best not to think of her too much. It hurt. It was too painful when he considered what he had done. It had never been her fault. It had always been his. He'd known the rules from the beginning and he'd thought he could do his own thing anyway.

'Good. You need to move on. More important things are coming up.'

He nodded. But he knew he would *never* forget her. How could he?

'You've got your robe fitting today, yes?'

The coronation robes needed adjusting for Matteo's broad form. 'Yes.'

'I might come along. It's been a long time since I saw those robes. My own coronation, in fact. That was a great day. Great memories. It'll be the same for you.'

'I'm sure it will.'

'You're sure you're all right? You seem very… *absent*.'

'Fine.'

'You'd tell me if there was something bothering you?'

'Of course!'

'Good. I'd hate to think you were keeping something from me, like before.'

'We never *kept* it from you, Papà. It was something new for both of us. We were trying to work it out for ourselves first.'

The King nodded as he hauled himself up from the table and then surprised his son by saying, 'Dr Szenac did seem a very nice woman. I'm sorry I had to force your hand, but I had to do it before you got in too deep. I couldn't bear the idea that you were going to get hurt further down the road, and neither was it very fair to her, when *you* knew the situation. I was surprised at you, son.'

Matteo stared at his father. 'We were already in too deep. We got hurt anyway.'

'I know what it's like to lose a loved one, Matteo. When I lost your mother, I...' He shook his head, clearing away the thought. 'Anyway, I did what I thought was best. For you. I only want the best for you.'

'*She* was the best, Papà. And I ruined it.'

Alberto nodded. 'I'm sorry.'

And he left his son sitting at the breakfast table, surrounded by a litter of pastry crumbs.

She'd been spending a lot of time in the nature reserve. It was just so peaceful out there and she'd managed to complete quite a few new paintings—including one of a sunset over the lake that had been astoundingly beautiful.

Decima-Malafede had been a comfort to her torn and broken soul, but after she'd packed the last of her canvases, checking out her room for one last time, Krystiana went downstairs, hugged the proprietors of the bed and breakfast, who had become good friends, and bade them goodbye.

It was time to go home.

Aunt Carolina had called with the news that repairs to her villa were complete and it was liveable again.

The news had been a nice surprise, but she'd felt a wave of sadness wash over her. Matteo had done that for her. Sorted out the villa. She'd kind of imagined, not too long ago, that they would both drive back there in one of the palace cars and look around the rebuild together. She'd briefly imagined putting the place up for sale, seeing as her new life was going to be based in the Grand Palace, the House of Romano.

None of that was to be. *What a fool!*

But she couldn't stay here, hiding away from life. Enough time had passed for her to be able to return, and hopefully the media would have moved on. Surely Matteo would have told them their relationship was over?

'They might still try to talk to you. Get the inside story on Matteo,' Aunt Carolina had warned.

But how could she stay away? She needed to return to work, and she needed, more than anything, to find her old routine. Her routine had kept her safe and secure. Unknown and unloved. That was the best way.

Handing over her key, she gave the owners a sad smile, thanked them for their care, their consideration and their silence, and then she walked out through the front door.

Wondering just what she might be walking back to.

Her villa felt strange. Hers, but not quite hers. Maybe because Bruno wasn't with her? She needed to collect him.

Krystiana set her bags down and slumped

onto the sofa, feeling apprehensive at being back. There'd been no press on her doorstep. Had they given up? Figured she was gone? She hoped so.

With nothing better to do, she reached for the remote and switched on the television. As it came to life she heard the voice of the newscaster mentioning that the Crown Prince of Isla Tamoura was now King Matteo Romano, after his coronation earlier that day.

No wonder there aren't any press at my door.

She stared at the images of him on the throne, red ermine-trimmed robes around him, as he held the sceptre and orb, a crown of gold and jewels upon his head.

He looked very regal. And handsome.

She sucked in a sudden breath, the loss almost too much to bear.

She didn't know how to feel. Her heart was breaking so painfully. How was it still so raw?

She grabbed the remote and turned off the television, trying to wipe the images from her brain as she began to cry, holding a cushion in front of her as if its very presence might somehow cushion the force of the pain racing through her once again.

It was like a thorn in her side. A pain twisting deep in her heart.

He'd moved on.

Without her.

Clearly he had accepted the duty he was meant for and she wanted to be happy for him. But…

It hurt. More than she'd believed possible.

Krystiana cried herself to sleep, still holding the cushion like a shield.

'You thought I wouldn't find out?'

'Find out what?' Matteo sipped calmly from his espresso.

'Don't be coy with me, Matteo. You *know* what I'm talking about! The law that now allows you to marry a commoner!'

Matteo wiped his mouth with a napkin as he shook his head. He'd thought about this a lot. Thought about what was right. And what he knew was this—he loved Krystiana. He would never find such a connection again. His entire happiness had been destroyed by a law that was archaic and out of date, and he'd been determined that his first order of business as King was to get it changed.

His entire life had been empty since she'd left and his heart had *ached.* He had fought against himself more than anyone else, in deciding to do this. Nothing might come of it—she might never forgive him—but he had to try.

'You want me to be a king who leads his country into the future, yes?' he said now.

'Of course!'

'Well, in that case I take it upon myself to change a few things. Make this a new, modern monarchy. We need to move with the times if we want our people to relate to us and respect us.'

'Are you going after her?'

Matteo stared at his father. Wasn't it obvious?

'Yes. If she'll have me.'

He expected his father to rant and rave, to argue that a king should never debase himself by begging for a woman's affections, but surprisingly he did not.

Instead, his voice was low and gentle. 'She means this much to you?'

'I love her and I've been miserable without her here. Couldn't you tell?'

His father nodded. 'Yes. I could.'

'You lost Mamma years ago. But if you could have a chance to get her back wouldn't you take it?'

His father stared at him, his eyes softening, welling up with tears. 'Yes.'

'Well, then… Would you deny me the love of my life? Knowing how it feels to be lost without her?'

'No. I would not deny you. You must love her very much to have done this.'

'I do.'

He stepped forward to clasp his son and pat him on the back. 'Then you have my blessing.'

Matteo was surprised. 'Really?'

'I've seen how you've been since she's been gone, and quite frankly you're almost back to how you were after you first came home after the kidnapping. You have no life in you. No joy. The only time I see you happy is when you are with Alex. I wasn't the right king to challenge the rules, but you *are*. Like you say—it's the future.'

'Thank you,' he said, feeling emotional. 'That means more than I can say.'

'Do you think you can bring her back?'

'I don't know. But it was never about the law keeping us apart. It was about me not telling her the truth. I'll need her to put her trust in me and I'm not sure if she will.'

'Well, call me when you know for sure.'

'I will. Thank you, Papà.'

'Good luck, son.'

CHAPTER THIRTEEN

AFTER A LONG day at work—and it had been a *long* day—there was nothing Krystiana loved more than to walk along the beach, barefoot, watching Bruno frolic in the sea. There was peace out here, freedom. *Anonymity.*

She'd spent the last few weeks fielding questions from her patients, trying to move them back to the topic of themselves rather than her and her fleeting romance with their King. It had been hard denying that there was anything going on, and every time someone questioned her about it it was like being stabbed in the heart again as she told them that, no, she and the King were not together. That it had simply been a friendly meal together and the press had misconstrued it.

It was exhausting, quite frankly—so much so that she was even considering moving elsewhere. Maybe starting her own medical practice...perhaps in Rome or Florence? Somewhere far away from here.

But she'd already fled from one home. She didn't want to have to flee another. She loved this island so much.

Bruno yapped with happiness as he brought her over a ball he'd found and dropped it at her feet. She picked it up and threw it as far as she could, smiling as he chased after it. She couldn't take him away from this, either.

She looked out to sea, watching a white yacht in the distance. It looked so calm and peaceful. So pretty. Almost worth painting.

But she didn't have her easel or paints. It was just herself and her dog.

And that's all it's ever going to be.

Matteo's anxiety levels soared once he got into the car that would take him to Krystiana's villa. He knew she was back. He'd been notified the second she came back, her ID having flagged up a special program in the airport.

When his secretary had told him he'd had to fight the urge to go after her straight away, knowing there was no point in doing so until the new law had been passed. He wanted to present it as a *fait accompli*.

He'd missed her so much, and when he'd learnt that she had flown to Rome he'd wondered if she was ever going to come back. But she had, and he had taken some comfort in knowing that she was back on the island. He had stood each evening on his balcony, looking out towards where he knew her villa was, imagining that she was looking at the palace on the hill so far away...

It was a romantic notion, he knew, and probably a bit silly, but it was because he was heartsick, missing her like crazy. He knew that once he saw her again he would be able to tell her everything he had been doing. He would apologise profusely and hopefully—*hopefully*—she would take him back.

But she might not. He'd hurt her—he knew that—and she might not want to risk that again. Plus there'd be the whole thing of being back in the public eye again. He'd already ordered the press to stay away from her villa and her place of work, to give her some chance of returning to normal. He'd even taken one newspaper to court, taken legal action against them harassing her, and thankfully they'd obeyed the order.

Everyone missed her. Mara wanted her back. Alex talked about her. Well, mostly it was about Bruno, but still...

As the sleek, dark vehicle pulled to a halt outside her refurbished villa he felt the butterflies in his stomach all launch into flight at once. His heart pounded, his mouth and throat went very dry, and it took him a few moments to get out of the car. When he did, his legs felt as if they would go out from under him.

He was met with a flashback of what the place had looked like after the crash. The debris, the rubble… The accident that had caused their love to happen.

It was weird how life worked. If there'd been no accident she wouldn't have stayed at the palace and he wouldn't have got to know her, to fall in love with her.

He glanced at the windows. Had she seen him yet?

Straightening his jacket, he walked up to the door and knocked, his heart hammering, sweat beading his armpits.

There was no answer. So he knocked again.

A silver-haired head popped up over the fence next door. 'Hello? Are you after Krystiana? Oh, my God! It's *you*!' The head disappeared as the woman next door curtsied. 'Your Majesty!'

'Has she gone out?'

'She doesn't get back until late these days.'

'Where is she? Work?'

'No, no. She goes down to the beach with the dog.'

He turned to look down at the long sweep of golden sand far in the distance. 'That beach?'

'I guess so. I'm not sure.'

'Thank you. What's your name?'

'Anna.'

'Thank you, Anna. I would be grateful if you didn't mention this visit to anyone just yet.'

'Of course not.' She made a zipping motion across her lips and smiled.

He smiled his thanks. A reprieve. A moment or two in which he could gather himself some more.

He got back into the car and gave the order to his driver. 'Take me to the beach.'

'Yes, sir.' And the driver fired the engine.

Sitting on the sand, looking out to sea, as she often did, she thought about all that had happened in her life to bring her to this spot. The quirks of fate. The actions of others and how they could impact on your own life and the choices you had to make.

If she'd not been part of Dr Bonetti's practice... If her Aunt Carolina had lived somewhere else... If her parents hadn't divorced...

No wonder she wanted as much control over her own life as she could get.

She was sitting there, drizzling sand through her fingers, when she felt a prickling on the back of her neck. As if she was being watched.

Krystiana turned around...curious, cautious... her heartbeat increasing slightly, searching for a pair of eyes, hoping to brush it off as a flight of fancy, or that perhaps it was just another dog-walker, or a fisherman come down to the coast.

But it wasn't a dogwalker or a fisherman.

It was a king.

Matteo stood tall and proud, his dark form silhouetted against the sun as he walked across the sand directly towards her. She scrambled to her feet, dusting off the sand from her clothes, her heart thudding away like a jackhammer.

Why was he here? After all this time?

What was left for them to say to each other?

Far behind him, blocking access to the beach, were security guards so they could have privacy. She saw their dark-suited forms, the sun glancing off their sunglasses.

She fought the need to run towards him, to fall into his arms. But her love for him had almost broken her so she held firm, letting him come to *her*. If he was here to make an apology, then he could do all the work.

He looked as handsome as ever. Maybe even more so. Was he taller? Or was it just a different bearing he had? That somehow becoming King had changed him?

'*Buonasera*, Matteo.'

'*Dobyr wieczór*, Krystiana.'

She was surprised to hear her own language. 'You learned Polish?'

'A little.'

'That's good.' She sucked in a huge breath. 'What brings you here?'

'I came to ask for your forgiveness.'

Forgiveness?

Krystiana's heart almost leapt from her chest. 'Why?'

'Because I love you and I can't live without you.'

Her cheeks flushed with heat at his words. Words she'd longed to hear him say, but words that put daggers into her heart. Why was he doing this? They couldn't be together! It was torture.

She looked down and away. 'Let's not go through this again.'

'I want you to come back with me, Krystiana,' he said.

No! Please don't say that to me! I can't go through this heartbreak!

'Matteo, no—'

'I changed the law.'

She looked up at him, shocked, her heart thudding. 'What?'

'I changed the law about kings not being allowed to marry who they wish. And even if it had been impossible for me to change it I would have come and fetched you anyway. We could have lived in sin.' He smiled.

She stared at him, open-mouthed. Surely he was joking? He'd changed something that had been practically written in stone since his country had begun writing its history? For *her*?

But it didn't matter what he'd done. The law wasn't the point. His lying to her was what had been the fault.

'But…'

'I'm sorry. So, so sorry! For hurting you. For making you think that I had lied to you.'

'You did.'

'But I didn't mean to! I was confused. Torn by everything that I was feeling for you. I kept trying to fight it, but I couldn't, and before I knew what was happening we were getting serious and— '

'Are you blaming *me* for this?'

'No! Absolutely not! You're blameless. I tried to make it feel as if it was your fault, but no, it was all mine. I knew what it would do to you and yet I still did it. I should have thought about how much you needed me to show you that I could be trusted, that I could be relied upon and I can be all those things! Because I'm thinking more clearly now than I have in my entire life!' He paused to gather himself again. 'I love you and I want to show the world that, and I want you to see that I also acted from a place of fear. Something I found hard to admit to myself. I'm a king. I was a prince. I never thought I'd want anyone ever again after my kidnapping and then you walked into my life. I tried to fight it. I did. I think you did, too. But something kept pulling us together and I'd already been through so much, I thought to myself that I could allow myself this brief moment of happiness and to hell with the consequences! I thought we could deal with them later.'

'Until your hand was forced.'

He nodded. 'I don't expect you to forgive me. Or to trust me. Not at first. But I am begging you and I will get on my hands and knees to ask you to give me the chance, again, to show you who I really am.'

'Who are you?' she asked, her voice almost trembling.

'A man who loves you. Who wants to marry you and keep you in my life for ever, until death do us part.'

It was everything she wanted to hear. And she wanted to trust him, so much!

'Your father hates me, we—'

'My father doesn't hate you. He was trying to protect me from getting hurt further down the line. Not realising how much we were already in love! But now he knows and he has given us his blessing.'

She was in shock. Not sure what to say. 'He has?'

'Yes. I'm sorry, Krystiana. Sorry I wasn't strong

enough to do this in the first place. To have fought
for you. But I couldn't do anything to change the
law until I became King myself. Then I could put
forward a new decree. These things take time,
needing approval from my parliament, all that
nonsense, and I couldn't tell you what I was doing,
because I didn't want to give you false hope if I
failed.'

He stepped forward, tucked a windblown tress
of hair behind her ear. 'There could never be anyone else but you. It's always been you, Krystiana.
Let me show you the truth of my love. The truth
of my heart. That you can put your life and your
heart into my hands and I will keep them safe.
That I will cherish you and adore you for ever-
more.' And he made to kiss her.

She thought for just a moment. Hesitated, but
then she closed her eyes in ecstasy as his lips
touched hers and somehow, before she knew it,
her arms were around his neck and she was pulling him close, revelling in being with him, kissing him, holding him, once again.

He had changed the law for her. And he was
trying so hard to explain why he had acted the
way that he had. And she could forgive him for
that, because she'd known he'd been just as confused as she.

They could be together! She melted into the
kiss, sinking against him.

'Are you sure you want me?' she asked him breathlessly. 'I'm complicated and I have faults and I get mad quickly and I—'

He smiled, laughing. 'I do.' And then he let her go, so that he could get down on one knee.

Reaching into his pocket, he pulled out a small red box, something that he had bought a long time ago, but had never had the chance to use. Opening it, he revealed a beautiful diamond solitaire ring, that winked and glittered in the low evening sun. Bruno dropped his ball, as if sensing the moment and came to sit by Matteo's side, looking questioningly at them both.

'Krystiana Szenac. You brought light into my life. Gave me hope where there was none and I cannot live without you. I love you so much! Will you do me the honour of becoming my Queen?'

Krystiana gasped, laughing.

He was looking up at her, smiling, hope in his eyes and she knew instantly where she wanted to be.

At his side.

'Yes! I will!' She held out her hand so that he could slide on the ring and it fitted perfectly! She gazed at it in awe, then she pulled him to his feet and kissed him.

The beach melted away, her sorrow melted away. Perhaps happiness did eventually come to those that waited?

She'd never thought so much joy could come from so much heartbreak.

Never thought that that amount of joy, could ever be hers.

EPILOGUE

'Is THIS ALL RIGHT?' Krystiana tried to speak
without breaking her smile as she gave her newly
learned royal wave from the car touring through
Tamoura.

Matteo glanced at her and smiled. 'It's perfect. As are you.'

They were travelling in a convoy of security,
in front and behind of their car were mounted
soldiers in their finery, the horses' hooves clip-
clopping along the roads as Matteo and Krystiana and Alex were driven through streets filled
with adoring, cheering crowds.

In front of them, Alex waved madly from a
window, enjoying being the centre of attention,
but after a mile or so of doing the same thing,
the little girl got a bit bored and she sat beside
Krystiana and laid a hand on her stepmother's
barely swollen belly.

'When is the baby coming?' she asked. 'Today?'

Krystiana smiled at her stepdaughter and

stroked her cheek lovingly. 'Not today, darling. Many more sleeps before the baby arrives.'

Alex sat back in her seat. 'I want a girl.'

'Do you? We'll have to wait and see. It could be a boy *or* a girl. Now, wave, *mio caro.* The people want to see you.'

She smiled at Matteo and clutched his hand with her own, squeezing it tightly. It had been almost two years since Matteo had arrived on that beach to ask for her hand in marriage and since then so much had happened. So much had changed!

They'd got married in a beautiful cathedral, with the ceremony nationally televised. They'd honeymooned in the Caribbean, and when they'd returned home to begin their royal duties together Krystiana had discovered that she was pregnant with his child.

And life as *Queen* was everything she had hoped it would be. She wasn't just a figurehead. She wasn't just her husband's wife. She was a pioneer, bringing her work and experience to the forefront, opening up clinics and bringing awareness for those who had been abused, held hostage or kept as slaves. The press loved her and she made sure she used every public opportunity that she could to help those that were less fortunate.

She was still doing good.

Still helping.

And her heart was filled with love and hope for the future.

She wasn't alone any more.

The darkness and the fear were gone.

And love and light filled her heart every day.

* * * * *

*If you enjoyed this story, check out
these other great reads from
Louisa Heaton*

Their Unexpected Babies
Saving the Single Dad Doc
A Child to Heal Them
Pregnant with His Royal Twins

All available now!